The Mother

Norman Duncan

Illustrated by H. E. Fritz

The Mother

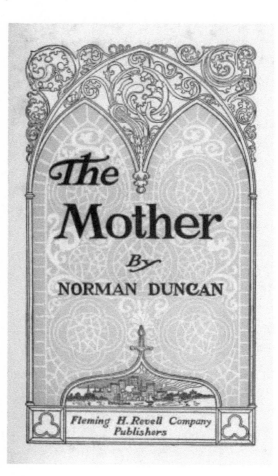

The
Mother

By

NORMAN DUNCAN

Fleming H. Revell Company
Publishers

The Mother

by

Norman Duncan

1905

The Decorations
In This Book Were
Designed by H. E. Fritz

CONTENTS

The Mother

BY PROXY

It will be recalled without effort—possibly, indeed, without interest—that the obsequies of the old Senator Boligand were a distinguished success: a fashionable, proper function, ordered by the young widow with exquisite taste, as all the world said, and conducted without reproach, as the undertaker and the clergy very heartily agreed. At the Church of the Lifted Cross, the incident of the child, the blonde lady and the mysteriously veiled man, who sat in awe and bewildered amazement where the shadows gave deepest seclusion, escaped notice. Not that the late Senator Boligand was in life aware of the existence of the child or the lady or the strange fellow with the veil. Nothing of the sort. The one was the widow of Dick Slade, the other his son, born in wedlock; and the third was the familiar counsellor and intimate of them all. The Senator was for once turned to good account: was made contributor to the sweetness of life, to the comfort of the humble. That was all. And I fancy that the shade of the grim old robber, lurking somewhere in the softly coloured gloom of the chancel, was not altogether averse to the farce in which his earthly tabernacle was engaged....

When Dick Slade died in the big red tenement of Box Street, he died as other men die, complaining of the necessity; and his son, in the way of all tender children, sorely wept: not because his father was now lost to him, which was beyond his comprehension, but because the man must be put in a grave—a cold place, dark and suffocating, being underground, as the child had been told.

"I don't want my father," he woefully protested, "to be planted!"

"Planted!" cried the mother, throwing up her hands in indignant denial. "Who told you he'd be planted?"

"Madame Lacara."

"She's a liar," said the woman, composedly, without resentment. "We'll cut the *planting* out of *this* funeral." Her ingenuity, her resourcefulness, her daring, when the happiness of her child was concerned, were usually sufficient to the emergency. "Why, darling!" she exclaimed. "Your father will be taken right up into the sky. He won't be put in no grave. He'll go right straight to a place where it's all sunshine—where it's all blue and high and as bright as day." She bustled about: keeping an eye alert for the effect of her promises. She was not yet sure how this glorious ascension might be managed; but she had never failed to deceive him to his own contentment, and 'twas not her habit to take fainthearted measures. "They been lying to you, dear," she complained. "Don't you fret about graves. You just wait," she concluded, significantly, "and see!"

The boy sighed.

"Poddle and me," she added, with a wag of the head to convince him, "will show you where your father goes."

"I wish," the boy said, wistfully, "that he wasn't dead."

"Don't you do it!" she flashed. "It don't make no difference to him. It's a good thing. I bet he's glad to be dead."

The boy shook his head.

"Yes, he is! Don't you think he isn't. There ain't nothing like being dead. Everybody's happy—when they're dead."

"He's so still!" the boy whispered.

"It feels fine to be still—like that."

"And he's so cold!"

"No!" she scorned. "He don't feel cold. You think he's cold. But he ain't. That's just what you *think*. He's comfortable. He's glad to be dead. Everybody's glad to be dead."

The boy shuddered.

"Don't you do that no more!" said the woman. "It don't hurt to be dead. Honest, it don't! It feels real good to be that way."

"I—I—I don't think I'd like—to be dead!"

"You don't have to if you don't want to," the woman replied, thrown into a confusion of pain and alarm. To comfort him, to shield him from agony, to keep the shadow of fear from falling upon him: she desired nothing more; and she was content to succeed if but for the moment. "I tell you," she continued, "you never will be dead—if you don't want to. Your father wanted to be dead. 'I think, Millie,' says he, 'I'd like to be dead.' 'All right, Dick,' says I. 'If you want to, I won't stand in your way. But I don't know about the boy.' 'Oh,' says he, 'the boy won't stand in my way.' 'I guess that's right, Dick,' says I, 'for the boy loves you.' And so," she concluded, "he died. But *you* don't have to die. You'll never die—not unless you want to." She kissed him. "Don't you be afraid, dear!" she crooned.

"I'm not—afraid."

"Well, then," she asked, puzzled, "what *are* you?"

"I don't know," he faltered. "I think it makes me—sick at the—stomach."

He had turned white. She took him in her arms, to comfort and hearten him—an unfailing device: her kisses, her warm, ample bosom, her close embrace; he was by these always consoled....

Next day, then, in accordance with the woman's device, the boy and his mother set out with the veiled man for the Church of the Lifted Cross, where the obsequies of Senator Boligand were to take place. It was sad weather—a cold rain falling, the city gray, all the world

3

black-clad and dripping and sour of countenance. The veiled man said never a word; he held the boy's hand tight, and strode gloomily on—silent of melancholy, of protest, of ill temper: there was no knowing, for his face was hid. The woman, distinguished by a mass of blinding blonde hair and a complexion susceptible to change by the weather, was dressed in the ultra-fashionable way—the small differences of style all accentuated: the whole tawdry and shabby and limp in the rain. The child, a slender boy, delicately white of skin, curly headed, with round, dark eyes, outlooking in wonder and troubled regard, but yet bravely enough, trotted between the woman and the man, a hand in the hand of each.... And when they came to the Church of the Lifted Cross; and when the tiny, flickering lights, and the stained windows, and the shadows overhead, and the throbbing, far-off music had worked their spell upon him, he snuggled close to his mother, wishing himself well away from the sadness and mystery of the place, but glad that its solemn splendour honoured the strange change his father had chosen to undergo.

"Have they brought papa yet?" he whispered.

"Hush!" she answered. "He's come."

For a moment she was in a panic—lest the child's prattle, being perilously indiscreet, involve them all in humiliating difficulties. Scandal of this sort would be intolerable to the young Boligand widow.

"Where is he?"

"Don't talk so loud, dear. He's down in front—where all the lights are."

"Can't we go there?'

"No, no!" she whispered, quickly. "It isn't the way. We must sit here. Don't talk, dear; it isn't the way."

"I'd like to—kiss him."

"Oh, my!" she exclaimed. "It isn't allowed. We got to sit right here. That's the way it's always done. Hush, dear! Please don't talk."

With prayer and soulful dirges—employing white robes and many lights and the voices of children—the body of Senator Boligand was dealt with, in the vast, dim church, according to the forms prescribed, and with due regard for the wishes of the young widow. The Senator was an admirable substitute; Dick Slade's glorious ascension was accomplished. And the heart of the child was comforted by this beauty: for then he knew that his father was by some high magic admitted to the place of which his mother had told him—some place high and blue and ever light as day. The fear of death passed from him. He was glad, for his father's sake, that his father had died; and he wished that he, too, might some day know the glory to which his father had attained.

But when the earthly remains of the late distinguished Senator were borne down the aisle in solemn procession, the boy had a momentary return of grief.

"Is that papa in the box?" he whimpered.

His mother put her lips to his ear. "Yes," she gasped. "But don't talk. It isn't allowed."

The veiled man turned audibly uneasy. "Cuss it!" he fumed.

"Oh, father!" the boy sobbed.

With happy promptitude the veiled man acted. He put a hand over the boy's mouth. "For God's sake, Millie," he whispered to the woman, "let's get out of here! We'll be run in."

"Hush, dear!" the woman commanded: for she was much afraid.

After that, the child was quiet.

From the room in the Box Street tenement, meantime, the body of Dick Slade had been taken in a Department wagon to a resting-place befitting in degree.

"Millie," the veiled man protested, that night, "you didn't ought to fool the boy."

"It don't matter, Poddle," said she. "And I don't want him to feel bad."

"You didn't ought to do it," the man persisted. "It'll make trouble for him."

"I can't see him hurt," said the woman, doggedly. "I love him so much. Poddle, I just can't! It hurts *me*."

The boy was now in bed. "Mother," he asked, lifting himself from the pillow, "when will I die?"

"Why, child!" she ejaculated.

"I wish," said the boy, "it was to-morrow."

"There!" said the woman, in triumph, to the man. "He ain't afraid of death no more."

"I told you so, Millie!" the man exclaimed, at the same instant.

"But he ain't afraid to die," she persisted. "And that's all I want."

"You can't fool him always," the man warned.

The boy was then four years old....

THE RIVER

Top floor rear of the Box Street tenement looked out upon the river. It was lifted high: the activities of the broad stream and of the motley world of the other shore went silently; the petty noises of life—the creak and puff and rumble of its labouring machinery,—straying upward from the fussy places below, were lost in the space between.

Within: a bed, a stove, a table—the gaunt framework of home. But the window overlooked the river; and the boy was now seven years old, unknowing, unquestioning, serenely obedient to the circumstances of his life: feeling no desire that wandered beyond the familiar presence of his mother—her voice and touch and brooding love.

It was a magic window—a window turned lengthwise, broad, low, small-paned, disclosing wonders without end: a scene of infinite changes. There was shipping below, restless craft upon the water; and beyond, dwarfed in the distance, was a confusion of streets, of flat, puffing roofs, stretching from the shining river to the far, misty hills, which lay beside the sea, invisible and mysterious.

But top floor rear was remote from the river and the roofs. From the window—and from the love in the room—the boy looked out upon an alien world, heard the distant murmur, monotonously proceeding, night and day: uncomprehending, but unperturbed....

In the evening the boy sat with his mother at the window. Together they watched the shadows gather—the hills and the city and the river dissolve: the whole broad world turn to points of light, twinkling, flashing, darting, in the black, voiceless gulf. Nor would she fail to watch the night come, whether in gentle weather or whipping rain: but there would sit, the boy in her arms, held close to her breast, her hand straying restlessly over his small body, intimately caressing it.

The falling shadows; the river, flowing unfeelingly; the lights, wandering without rest, aimless, forever astray in the dark: these were a spell upon her.

"They go to the sea!" she whispered, once.

"The ships, mother?"

She put his head in the hollow of her shoulder, where her cheek might touch his hair: all the time staring out at the lights on the river.

"All the ships, all the lights on the river," she said, hoarsely, "go out there."

"Why?"

"The river takes them."

He was made uneasy: being conscious of the deeper meaning— acutely aware of some strange dread stirring in her heart.

"Maybe," he protested, "they're glad to go away."

She shook her head. "One night," she said, leaning towards the window, seeming now to forget the boy, "I seen the sea. All the lights on the river go different ways—when they get out there. It is a dark and lonesome place—big and dark and lonesome."

"Then," said he, quickly, "you would not like to be there."

"No," she answered. "I do not like the sky," she continued; "it is so big and empty. I do not like the sea; it is so big and dark. And black winds are always blowing there; and the lights go different ways. The lights," she muttered, "go different ways! I am afraid of the dark. And, oh!" she moaned, suddenly crushing him to her breast, rocking him, in an agony of tenderness, "I am afraid of something else. Oh, I am afraid!"

"Of what?" he gasped.

"To be alone!" she sobbed.

He released himself from her arms—sat back on her knee: quivering from head to foot, his hands clenched, his lips writhing. "Don't, mother!" he cried. "Don't cry. We will not go to the sea. We *will* not!"

"We must," she whispered.

"Oh, why?"

She kissed him: her hand slipped under his knees; and she drew him close again—and there held him until he lay quiet in her arms.

"We are like the lights on the river," she said. "The river will take us to a place where the lights go different ways."

"We will not go!"

"The river will take us."

The boy was puzzled: he lifted his head, to watch the lights drift past, far below; and he was much troubled by this mystery. She tried to gather his legs in her lap—to hold him as she used to do, when he was a child at her breast; but he was now grown too large for that, and she suffered, again, the familiar pain: a perception of alienation—of inevitable loss.

"When?" he asked.

She let his legs fall. "Soon," she sighed. "When you are older; it won't be long, now. When you are a little wiser; it will be very soon."

"When I am wiser," he pondered, "we must go. What makes me wiser?"

"The wise."

"Are you wise?"

"God help me!" she answered.

He nestled his head on her shoulder—dismissing the mystery with a quick sigh. "Never mind," he said, to comfort her. "You will not be alone. I will be with you."

"I wonder!" she mused.

For a moment more she looked out; but she did not see the river—but saw the wide sea, wind-tossed and dark, where the great multitude of lights went apart, each upon its mysterious way.

"Mother," he repeated, reproachfully, mystified by her hesitation, "I will always be with you."

"I wonder!" she mused.

To this doubt—now clear to him beyond hope—there was instant response: strangely passionate, but in keeping with his nature, as she knew. For a space he lay rigid on her bosom: then struggled from her embrace, brutally wrenching her hands apart, flinging off her arms. He stood swaying: his hands clenched, his slender body aquiver, as before, his dark eyes blazing reproach. It gave her no alarm, but, rather, exquisite pleasure, to watch his agony. She caught him by the shoulders, and bent close, that by the night-light, coming in at the window, she might look into his eyes: wherein, swiftly, the flare of

10

reproach turned to hopeless woe. And she was glad that he suffered: exalted, so that she, too, trembled.

"Oh," he pleaded, "say that I will always be with you!"

She would not: but continued to exult in his woeful apprehension.

"Tell me, mother!" he implored. "Tell me!"

Not yet: for there was no delight to be compared with the proved knowledge of his love.

"Mother!" he cried.

"You do not love me," she said, to taunt him.

"Oh, don't!" he moaned.

"No, no!" she persisted. "You don't love your mother any more."

He was by this reduced to uttermost despair; and he began to beat his breast, in the pitiful way he had. Perceiving, then, that she must no longer bait him, she opened her arms. He sprang into them. At once his sobs turned to sighs of infinite relief, which continued, until, of a sudden, he was hugged so tight that he had no breath left but to gasp.

"And you will always be with me?" he asked.

"It is the way of the world," she answered, while she kissed him, "that sons chooses for themselves."

With that he was quite content....

For a long time they sat silent at the window. The boy dreamed hopefully of the times to come — serenity restored. For the moment the woman was forgetful of the foreshadowed days, happy that the warm, pulsing little body of her son lay unshrinking in her arms: so conscious of his love and life—so wishful for a deeper sense of motherhood—that she slipped her hand under his jacket and felt about for his heart, and there let her fingers lie, within touch of its steady beating. The lights still twinkled and flashed and aimlessly wandered in the night; but the spell of the river was lifted.

A GARDEN OF LIES

Withal it was a rare mood: nor, being wise, was she given to expressing it in this gloomy fashion. It was her habit, rather, assiduously to woo him: this with kisses, soft and wet; with fleeting touches; with coquettish glances and the sly display of her charms; with rambling, fantastic tales of her desirability in the regard of men—thus practicing all the familiar fascinations of her kind, according to the enlightenment of the world she knew. He must be persuaded, she thought, that his mother was beautiful, coveted; convinced of her wit and gaiety: else he would not love her. Life had taught her no other way.... And always at break of day, when he awoke in her arms, she waited, with a pang of anxiety, pitilessly recurring, lest there be some sign that despite her feverish precautions the heedless world had in her nightly absence revealed that which she desperately sought to hide from him....

Thus, by and by, when the lamp was alight—when the shadows were all chased out of the window, driven back to the raw fall night, whence they had crept in—she lapsed abruptly into her natural manner and practices. She spread a newspaper on the table, whistling in a cheery fashion, the while covertly observing the effect of this lively behaviour. With a knowing smile, promising vast gratification, she got him on her knee; and together, cheek to cheek, her arm about his waist, they bent over the page: whereon some function of the rich, to which the presence of the Duchess of Croft and of the distinguished Lord Wychester had given sensational importance, was grotesquely pictured.

"Now, mother," said he, spreading the picture flat, "show me you."

"This here lady," she answered, evasively, "is the Duchess of Croft."

"Is it?" he asked, without interest. "She is very fat. Where are you?"

"And here," she proceeded, "is Lord Wychester."

"Mother," he demanded, "where are *you*?"

She was disconcerted; no promising evasion immediately occurred to her. "Maybe," she began, tentatively, "this lady here——"

"Oh, no!" he cried, looking up with a little laugh. "It is not like you, at all!"

"Well," she said, "it's probably meant for me."

He shook his head; and by the manner of this she knew that he would not be deceived.

"Perhaps," she said, "the Duchess told the man not to put me in the picture. I guess that's it. She was awful jealous. You see, dear," she went on, very solemnly, "Lord Wychester took a great fancy to me."

He looked up with interest.

"To—my shape," she added.

"Oh!" said he.

"And that," she continued, noting his pleasure, "made the Duchess hot; for *she's* too fat to have much of a figure. Most men, you know," she added, as though reluctant in her own praise, "do fancy mine." She brushed his cheek with her lips. "Don't you think, dear," she asked, assuming an air of girlish coquetry, thus to compel the compliment, "that I'm—rather—pretty?"

"I think, mother," he answered, positively, "that you're very, very pretty."

It made her eyes shine to hear it. "Well," she resumed, improvising more confidently, now, "the Duchess was awful mortified because Lord Wychester danced with me seventeen times. 'Lord Wychester,' says she, 'what *do* you see in that blonde with the diamonds?' 'Duchess,' says he, 'I bet the blonde don't weigh over a hundred and ten!'"

There was no answering smile; the boy glanced at the picture of the wise and courtly old Lord Wychester, gravely regarded that of the Duchess of Croft, of whose matronly charms, of whose charities and amiable qualities, all the world knows.

"What did she say?" he asked.

"'Oh, dear me, Lord Wychester!' says she. 'If you're looking for bones,' says she, 'that blonde is a regular glue-factory!'"

He caught his breath.

"'A regular glue-factory,'" she repeated, inviting sympathy. "That's what she said."

"Did you cry?"

"Not me!" she scorned. "Cry? Not me! Not for no mountain like her!"

"And what," he asked, "did Lord Wychester do?"

"'Back to the side-show, Duchess!' says Lord Wychester. 'You're too fat for decent company. My friend the Dook,' says he, 'may be partial to fat ladies and ten-cent freaks; but *my* taste runs to slim blondes.'"

No amusement was excited by Lord Wychester's second sally. In the world she knew, it would have provoked a shout of laughter. The boy's gravity disquieted her.

"Did you laugh?" he asked.

"Everybody," she answered, pitifully, "give her the laugh."

He sighed—somewhat wistfully. "I wish," he said, "that *you* hadn't."

"Why not!" she wondered, in genuine surprise.

"I don't know."

"Why, dear!" she exclaimed, a note of alarm in her voice. "It isn't bad manners! Anyhow," she qualified, quick to catch her cue, "I didn't laugh much. I hardly laughed at all. I don't believe I *did* laugh."

"I'm glad," he said.

Then, "I'm sure of it," she ventured, boldly; and she observed with relief that he was not incredulous.

"Did the Duchess cry?"

"Oh, my, no! 'Waiter,' says the Duchess, 'open another bottle of that wine. I feel faint.'"

"What did Lord Wychester do then?"

"He paid for the wine." It occurred to her that she might now surely delight him. "Then he wanted to buy a bottle for me," she continued, eagerly, "just to spite the Duchess. 'If *she* can have wine,' says he, 'there isn't no good reason why *you* got to go dry.' But I couldn't see it. 'Oh, come on!' says he. 'What's the matter with you? Have a drink.' 'No, you don't!' says I. 'Why not?' says he." She drew the boy a little closer, and, in the pause she patted his hand. "'Because,' says

I," she whispered, tenderly, "'I got a son; and I *don't want him to do no drinking when he grows up!*'" She paused again—that the effect of the words and of the caress might not be interrupted. "'Come off!' says Lord Wychester," she went on; "'you haven't got no son.' 'You wouldn't think to look at me,' says I, 'that I got a son seven years old the twenty-third of last month.' 'To the tall timber!' says he. 'You're too young and pretty. I'll give you a thousand dollars for a kiss.' 'No, you don't!' says I. 'Why not?' says he. 'Because,' says I, 'you don't.' 'I'll give you two thousand,' says he."

She was interrupted by the boy; his arms were anxiously stealing round her neck.

"'Three thousand!' says he."

"Mother," the boy whispered, "did you give it to him?"

Again, she drew him to her: as all mothers will, when, in the twilight, they tell tales to their children, and the climax approaches.

"'Four thousand!' says he."

"Mother," the boy implored, "tell me quick! What did you say?"

"'Lord Wychester,' says I, 'I don't give kisses,' says I, 'because my son doesn't want me to do no such thing! No, sir! Not for a million dollars!'"

She was then made happy by his rapturous affection; and she now first perceived—in a benighted way—that virtue was more appealing to him than the sum of her physical attractions. Upon this new thought she pondered. She was unable to reduce it to formal terms, to be sure; but she felt a new delight, a new hope, and was uplifted, though she knew not why. Later—at the crisis of their lives—the perception returned with sufficient strength to illuminate her way....

Presently the boy broke in upon her musing. "It was blondes Lord Wychester liked," he remarked, with pride; "wasn't it, mother?"

"Slim blondes," she corrected.

"Bleached blondes?"

She was appalled by the disclosure; and she was taken unaware: nor did she dare discover the extent, the significance, of this new sophistication, nor whence it came, lest she be all at once involved in a tangle of explanation, from which there could be no sure issue. She sighed; her head drooped, until it rested on his shoulder, her wet lashes against his cheek—despairing, helpless.

"What makes you sad?" he asked.

Then she gathered impetuous courage. She must be calm, she knew; but she must divert him. "See," she began, "what it says about your mother in the paper!" She ran her finger down a long column of the fulsome description of the great Multon ball—the list of fashionables, the costumes. "Here it is! 'She was the loveliest woman at the dance.' That's me. 'All the men said so. What if she is a bleached blonde? Some people says that bleached blondes is no good. It's a lie!'" she cried, passionately, to the bewilderment of the boy. "'God help them! There's honest people everywhere.' Are you listening? Here's more about me. 'She does the best she can. Maybe she *don't* amount to much, maybe she *is* a bleached blonde; but she does the best she can. She never done no wrong in all her life. She loves her son too much for that. Oh, she loves her son! She'd rather die than have him feel ashamed of her. There isn't a better woman in the world, There isn't a better mother — —'"

He clapped his hands.

"Don't you believe it?" she demanded. "Don't you believe what the paper says?"

"It's true!" he cried. "It's all true!"

The Mother

"How do you know," she whispered, intensely, "that it's all true?"

"I—just—*feel* it!"

They were interrupted by the clock. It struck seven times....

In great haste and alarm she put him from her knee; and she caught up her hat and cloak, and kissed him, and ran out, calling back her good-night, again and again, as she clattered down the stairs.... In the streets of the place to which she hurried, there were flaming lights, the laughter of men and flaunting women, the crash and rumble and clang of night-traffic, the blatant clamour of the pleasures of night; shuffling, blear-eyed derelicts of passion, creeping beldames, peevish children, youth consuming itself; rags and garish jewels, hunger, greasy content—a confusion of wretchedness, of greed and grim want, of delirious gaiety, of the sins that stalk in darkness.... Through it all she brushed, unconscious—lifted from it by the magic of this love: dwelling only upon the room that overlooked the river, and upon the child within; remembering the light in his eyes and the tenderness of his kiss.

THE CELEBRITY IN LOVE

While the boy sat alone, in wistful idleness, there came a knock at the door—a pompous rat-tat-tat, with a stout tap-tap or two added, once and for all to put the quality of the visitor beyond doubt. The door was then cautiously pushed ajar to admit the head of the personage thus impressively heralded. And a most extraordinary head it was— of fearsome aspect; nothing but long and intimate familiarity could resign the beholder to the unexpected appearance of it. Long, tawny hair, now sadly unkempt, fell abundantly from crown to shoulders; and hair as tawny, as luxuriantly thick, almost as long, completely covered the face, from every part of which it sprang, growing shaggy and rank at the eyebrows, which served to ambush two sharp little eyes: so that the whole bore a precise resemblance to an ill-natured Skye terrier. It is superfluous to add that this was at once the face and the fortune of Toto, the Dog-faced Man, known in private life, to as many intimates as a jealous profession can tolerate, as Mr. Poddle: for the present disabled from public appearance by the quality of the air supplied to the exhibits at Hockley's Musee, his lungs being, as he himself expressed it, "not gone, by no means, but gittin' restless."

"Mother gone?" asked the Dog-faced Man.

"She has gone, Mr. Poddle," the boy answered, "to dine with the Mayor."

"Oh!" Mr. Poddle ejaculated.

"Why do you say that?" the boy asked, frowning uneasily. "You always say, 'Oh!'"

"Do I? 'Oh!' Like that?"

"Why do you do it?"

"Celebrities," replied Mr. Poddle, testily, entering at that moment, "is not accountable. Me bein' one, don't ask me no questions."

"Oh!" said the boy.

Mr. Poddle sat himself in a chair by the window: and there began to catch and vent his breath; but whether in melancholy sighs or snorts of indignation it was impossible to determine. Having by these violent means restored himself to a state of feeling more nearly normal, he trifled for a time with the rings flashing on his thin, white fingers, listlessly brushed the dust from the skirt of his rusty frock coat, heaved a series of unmistakable sighs: whereupon—and by this strange occupation the boy was quite fascinated—he drew a little comb, a little brush, a little mirror, from his pocket; and having set up the mirror in a convenient place, he proceeded to dress his hair, with particular attention to the eyebrows, which, by and by, he tenderly braided into two limp little horns: so that 'twas not long before he looked much less like a frowsy Skye terrier, much more like an owl.

"The hour, Richard," he sighed, as he deftly parted his hair in the middle of his nose, "has came!"

With such fond and hopeless feeling were these enigmatical words charged that the boy could do nothing but heave a sympathetic sigh.

"You see before you, Richard, what you never seen before. A man in the clutches," Mr. Poddle tragically pursued, giving a vicious little twist to his left eyebrow, "of the tender passion!"

"Oh!" the boy muttered.

"'Fame,'" Mr. Poddle continued, improvising a newspaper head-line, to make himself clear, "'No Shield Against the Little God's Darts.' Git me? The high and the low gits the arrows in the same place."

"Does it—hurt?"

"Hurt!" cried Mr. Poddle, furiously. "It's perfectly excrugiating! Hurt? Why——"

"Mr. Poddle, excuse me," the boy interrupted, "but you are biting your mustache."

"Thanks," said Mr. Poddle, promptly. "Glad to know it. Can't afford to lose no more hirsute adornment. And I'm give to ravagin' it in moments of excitement, especially sorrow. Always tell me."

"I will," the boy gravely promised.

"The Pink-eyed Albino," Mr. Poddle continued, now released from the necessity of commanding his feelings, in so far as the protection of his hair was concerned, "was fancy; the Circassian Beauty was fascination; the Female Sampson was the hallugination of sky-blue tights; but the Mexican Sword Swallower," he murmured, with a melancholy wag, "is——"

"Mr. Poddle," the boy warned, "you are—at it again."

"Thanks," said Mr. Poddle, hastily eliminating the danger. "What I was about to remark," was his lame conclusion, "was that the Mexican Sword Swallower is *love*."

"Oh!"

The Dog-faced Man snapped a sigh in two. "Richard," he insinuated suspiciously, "what you sayin', 'Oh!' for?"

"Wasn't the Bearded Lady, love?"

"Love!" laughed Mr. Poddle. "Ha, ha! Far from it! Not so! The Bearded Lady was the snare of ambition. 'Marriage Arranged Between the Young Duke of Blueblood and the Daughter of the Clothes-pin King. Millions of the Higgleses to Repair the Duke's Shattered Fortunes.' Git me? 'Wedding of the Bearded Lady and the Dog-faced Man. Sunday Afternoon at Hockley's Popular Musee. No Extra Charge for Admission. Fabulous Quantity of Human Hair on Exhibition At the Same Instant. Hirsute Wonders To Tour the Country at Enormous Expense.' Git me? Same thing. Love? Ha, ha! Not so! There's no more love in *that*," Mr. Poddle concluded, bitterly, "than — —"

"Mr. Poddle, you are — —"

"Thanks," faltered Mr. Poddle. "As I was about to remark when you—ah—come to the rescue—love is froze out of high life. Us natural phenomenons is the slaves of our inheritages."

"But you said the Bearded Lady was love at last!"

"'Duke Said To Be Madly In Love With the American Beauty,'" Mr. Poddle composedly replied.

"I don't quite—get you?"

"Us celebrities has our secrets. High life is hollow. Public must be took into account. 'Sacrificed On His Country's Altar.' Git me? 'Good of the Profession.' Broken hearts—and all that."

"Would you have broken the Bearded Lady's heart?"

Mr. Poddle was by this recalled to his own lamentable condition. "I've gone and broke my own," he burst out; "for I'm give to understand that the lovely Sword Swallower is got entangled with a tattooed man. Not," Mr. Poodle hastily added, "with a *real* tattooed man! Not by no means! Far from it! *He's only half done!* Git me? His legs is finished; and I'm give to understand that the Chinese dragon on his back is gettin' near the end of its tail. There *may* be a risin' sun on his chest, and a snake drawed out on his waist; of that I've heard rumors, but I ain't had no reports. Not," said Mr. Poddle, impressively, "what you might call undenigeable reports. And Richard," he whispered, in great excitement and contempt, "that there half-cooked freak won't be done for a year! He's bein' worked over on the installment plan. And I'm give to understand that she'll wait! Oh, wimmen!" the Dog-faced Man apostrophized. "Took by shapes and complexions — —"

"Mr. Poddle, excuse me," the boy interrupted, diffidently, "but your eyebrow — —"

"Thanks," Mr. Poddle groaned, his frenzy collapsing. "As I was about to say, wimmen is like arithmetic; there ain't a easy sum in the book."

"Mr. Poddle!"

"Thanks," said Mr. Poddle, in deep disgust. "Am I at it again? O'erwhelming grief! This here love will be the ruin of me. 'Bank Cashier Defaulted For a Woman.' I've lost more priceless strands since I seen that charming creature than I'll get back in a year. I've bit 'em off! I've tore 'em out! If this here goes on I'll be a Hairless Wonder in a month. 'Suicided For Love.' Same thing exactly. And what's worse," he continued, dejectedly, "the objeck of my adoration don't look at it right. She takes me for a common audience. No regard for talent. No appreciation for hair in the wrong place. 'Genius Jilted By A Factory Girl.' And she takes that manufactured article of a tattooed man for a regular platform attraction! Don't seem to *know*, Richard, that freaks is born, not made. What's fame, anyhow?"

The boy did not know.

"Why, cuss me!" the Dog-faced Man exploded, "she treats me as if I was dead-headed into the Show!"

"Excuse me, but — —"

"Thanks. God knows, Richard, I ain't in love with her throat and stummick. It ain't because the one's unequalled for resistin' razor-edged steel and the other stands unrivalled in its capacity for holdin' cold metal. It ain't her talent, Richard. No, it ain't her talent. It ain't her beauty. It ain't even her fame. It ain't so much her massive proportions. It's just the way she darns stockings. Just the way she sits up there on the platform darnin' them stockings as if there wasn't no such thing as an admirin' public below. It's just her *self*. Git me? 'Give Up A Throne To Wed A Butcher's Daughter.' Understand? Why, God bless you, Richard, if she was a Fiji Island Cannibal I'd love her just the same!"

"I think, Mr. Poddle," the boy ventured, "that I'd tell her."

"I did," Mr. Poddle replied. "Much to my regrets I did. I writ. Worked up a beautiful piece out of 'The Lightning Letter-writer for Lovers.' 'Oh, beauteous Sword-Swallower,' I writ, 'pet of the public, pride of the sideshow, bright particular star in the constellation of natural phenomenons! One who is not unknown to fame is dazzled by your charms. He dares to lift his stricken eyes, to give vent to the tumultuous beatings of his manly bosom, to send you, in fact, this note. And if you want to know who done it, wear a red rose to-night.' Well," Mr. Poddle continued, "she seen me give it to the peanut-boy. And knowin' who it come from, she writ back. She writ," Mr. Poddle dramatically repeated, "right back."

The pause was so long, so painful, that the boy was moved to inquire concerning the answer.

"It stabs me," said Mr. Poddle.

"I think I'd like to know," said the boy.

"'Are you much give,' says she, 'to barkin' in your sleep?'"

A very real tear left the eye of Mr. Poddle, ran down the hair of his cheek, changed its course to the eyebrow, and there hung glistening....

It was apparent that the Dog-faced Man's thoughts must immediately be diverted into more cheerful channels. "Won't you please read to me, Mr. Poddle," said the boy, "what it says in the paper about my mother?"

The ruse was effective. Mr. Poddle looked up with a start. "Eh?" he ejaculated.

"Won't you?" the boy begged.

"I been talkin' so much, Richard," Mr. Poddle stammered, turning hoarse all at once, "that I gone and lost my voice."

He decamped to his room across the hall without another word.

AT MIDNIGHT

At midnight the boy had long been sound asleep in bed. The lamp was turned low. It was very quiet in the room—quiet and shadowy in all the tenement.... And the stair creaked; and footfalls shuffled along the hall—and hesitated at the door of the place where the child lay quietly sleeping; and there ceased. There was the rumble of a man's voice, deep, insistent, imperfectly restrained. A woman protested. The door was softly opened; and the boy's mother stepped in, moving on tiptoe, and swiftly turned to bar entrance with her arm.

"Hist!" she whispered, angrily. "Don't speak so loud. You'll wake the boy."

"Let me in, Millie," the man insisted. "Aw, come on, now!"

"I can't, Jim. You know I can't. Go on home now. Stop that! I won't marry you. Let go my arm. You'll wake the boy, I tell you!"

There was a short scuffle: at the end of which, the woman's arm still barred the door.

"Here I ain't seen you in three year," the man complained. "And you won't let me in. That ain't right, Millie. It ain't kind to an old friend like me. You didn't used to be that way."

"No," the woman whispered, abstractedly; "there's been a change. I ain't the same as I used to be."

"You ain't changed for the better, Millie. No, you ain't."

"I don't know," she mused. "Sometimes I think not. It ain't because I don't want you, Jim," she continued, speaking more softly, now, "that I don't let you in. God knows, I like to meet old friends; but— —"

It was sufficient. The man gently took her arm from the way. He stepped in—glanced at the sleeping boy, lying still as death, shaded from the lamp—and turned again to the woman.

"Don't wake him!" she said.

They were still standing. The man was short, long-armed, vastly broad at the shoulders, deep-chested: flashy in dress, dull and kind of feature—handsome enough, withal. He was an acrobat. Even in the dim light, he carried the impression of great muscular strength— of grace and agility. For a moment the woman's eyes ran over his stocky body: then, spasmodically clenching her hands, she turned quickly to the boy on the bed; and she moved back from the man, and thereafter regarded him watchfully.

"Don't make no difference if I do wake him," he complained. "The boy knows me."

"But he don't like you."

"Aw, Millie!" said he, in reproach. "Come off!"

"I seen it in his eyes," she insisted.

The man softly laughed.

"Don't you laugh no more!" she flashed. "You can't tell a mother what she sees in her own baby's eyes. I tell you, Jim, he don't like you. He never did."

"That's all fancy, Millie. Why, he ain't seen me in three year! And you can't see nothing in the eyes of a four year old kid. You're too fond of that boy, anyhow," the man continued, indignantly. "What's got into you? You ain't forgot that winter night out there in Idaho, have you? Don't you remember what you said to Dick that night? You said Dick was to blame, Millie, don't you remember? Remember the doctor coming to the hotel? I'll never forget how you went on. Never heard a woman swear like you before. Never seen one go on like you went on. And when you hit Dick, Millie, for what you said he'd done, I felt bad for Dick, though I hadn't much cause to care for what happened to him. Millie, girl, you was a regular wildcat when the doctor told you what was coming. You didn't want no kid, then!"

"Don't!" she gasped. "I ain't forgot. But I'm changed, Jim—since then."

He moved a step nearer.

"I ain't the same as I used to be in them days," she went on, staring at the window, and through the window to the starry night. "And Dick's dead, now. I don't know," she faltered; "it's all sort of—different."

"What's gone and changed you, Millie?"

"I ain't the same!" she repeated.

"What's changed you?"

"And I ain't been the same," she whispered, "since I got the boy!"

In the pause, he took her hand. She seemed not to know it—but let it lie close held in his great palm.

"And you won't have nothing to do with me?" he asked.

"I can't," she answered. "I don't think of myself no more. And the boy—wouldn't like it."

"You always said you would, if it wasn't for Dick; and Dick ain't here no more. There ain't no harm in loving me now." He tried to draw her to him. "Aw, come on!" he pleaded. "You know you like me."

She withdrew her hand—shrank from him. "Don't!" she said. "I like you, Jim. You know I always did. You was always good to me. I never cared much for Dick. Him and me teamed up pretty well. That was all. It was always you, Jim, that I cared for. But, somehow, now, I wish I'd loved Dick—more than I did. I feel different, now. I wish— oh, I wish—that I'd loved him!"

The man frowned.

"He's dead," she continued. "I can't tell him nothing, now. The chance is gone. But I wish I'd loved him!"

"He never done much for you."

"Yes, he did, Jim!" she answered, quickly. "He done all a man can do for a woman!"

She was smiling—but in an absent way. The man started. There was a light in her eyes he had never seen before.

"He give me," she said, "the boy!"

"You're crazy about that kid," the man burst out, a violent, disgusted whisper. "You're gone out of your mind."

"No, I ain't," she replied, doggedly. "I'm different since I got him. That's all. And I'd like Dick to know that I look at him different since he died. I can't love Dick. I never could. But I could thank him if he was here. Do you mind what I called the boy? I don't call him Claud now. I call him—Richard. It's all I can do to show Dick that I'm grateful."

The man caught his breath—in angry impatience. "Millie," he warned, "the boy'll grow up."

She put her hands to her eyes.

"He'll grow up and leave you. What you going to do then?"

"I don't know," she sighed. "Just—go along."

"You'll be all alone, Millie."

"He loves me!" she muttered. "He'll never leave me!"

"He's got to, Millie. He's got to be a man. You can't keep him."

"Maybe I *can't* keep him," she replied, in a passionate undertone. "Maybe I *do* love you. Maybe he'd get to love you, too. But look at him, Jim! See where he lies?"

The man turned towards the bed.

"It's on my side, Jim! Understand? He lies there always till I come in. Know why?"

He watched her curiously.

"He'll wake up, Jim, when I lift him over. That's what he wants. He'll wake up and say, 'Is that you, mother?' And he'll be asleep again, God bless him! before I can tell him that it is. My God! Jim, I can't tell you what it means to come in at night and find him lying there. That little body of a man! That clean, white soul! I can't tell you how I feel, Jim. It's something a man can't know. And do you think he'd stand for you? He'd say he would. Oh, he'd say he would! He'd look in my eyes, Jim, and he'd find out what I wanted him to say; and he'd *say* it. But, Jim, he'd be hurt. Understand? He'd think I

31

didn't love him any more. He's only a child—and he'd think I didn't love him. Where'd he sleep, Jim? Alone? He couldn't do it. Don't you *see*? I can't live with nobody, Jim. And I don't want to. I don't care for myself no more. I used to, in them days—when you and me and Dick and the crowd was all together. But I don't—no more!"

The man stooped, picked a small stocking from the floor, stood staring at it.

"I'm changed," the woman repeated, "since I got the boy."

"I don't know what you'll do, Millie, when he grows up."

She shook her head.

"And when he finds out?"

"That's what I'm afraid of," she whispered, hoarsely. "Somebody'll tell him—some day. He don't know, now. And I don't want him to know. He ain't our kind. Maybe it's because I keep him here alone. Maybe it's because he don't see nobody. Maybe it's just because I love him so. I don't know. But he ain't like us. It would hurt him to know. And I can't hurt him. I can't!"

The man tossed the stocking away. It fell upon a heap of little under-garments, strewn upon the floor.

"You're a fool, Millie," said he. "I tell you, he'll leave you. He'll leave you cold—when he grows up—and another woman comes along."

She raised her hand to stop him. "Don't say that!" she moaned. "There won't be no other woman. There can't be. Seems to me I'll want to kill the first that comes. A woman? What woman? There won't be none."

"There's *got* to be a woman."

"What woman? There ain't a woman in the world fit to—oh," she broke off, "don't talk of *him*—and a woman!"

"It'll come, Millie. He's a man—and there's got to be a woman. And she won't want you. And you'll be too old, then, to— —"

The boy stirred.

"Hist!" she commanded.

They waited. An arm was tossed—the boy smiled—there was a sigh. He was sound asleep again.

"Millie!" The man approached. She straightened to resist him. "You love me, don't you?"

She withdrew.

"You want to marry me?"

Still she withdrew; but he overtook her, and caught her hand. She was now driven to a corner—at bay. Her face was flushed; there was an irresolute light in her eyes—the light, too, of fear.

"Go 'way!" she gasped. "Leave me alone!"

He put his arm about her.

"Don't!" she moaned. "You'll wake the boy."

"Millie!" he whispered.

"Let me go, Jim!" she protested, weakly. "I can't. Oh, leave me alone! You'll wake the boy. I can't. I'd like to. I—I—I want to marry you; but I— —"

"Aw, come on!" he pleaded, drawing her close. And he suddenly found her limp in his arms. "You got to marry me!" he whispered, in triumph. "By God! you can't help yourself. I got you! I got you!"

"Oh, let me go!"

"No, I won't, Millie. I'll never let you go."

"For God's sake, Jim! Jim—oh, don't kiss me!"

The boy stirred again—and began to mutter in his sleep. At once the woman commanded herself. She stiffened—released herself—pushed the man away. She lifted a hand—until the child lay quiet once more. There was meantime breathless silence. Then she pointed imperiously to the door. The man sullenly held his place. She tiptoed to the door—opened it; again imperiously gestured. He would not stir.

"I'll go," he whispered, "if you tell me I can come back."

The boy awoke—but was yet blinded by sleep; and the room was dim-lit. He rubbed his eyes. The man and the woman stood rigid in the shadow.

"Is it you, mother?"

There was no resisting her command—her flashing eyes, the passionate gesture. The man moved to the door, muttering that he would come back—and disappeared. She closed the door after him.

"Yes, dear," she answered. "It is your mother."

"Was there a man with you?"

"It was Lord Wychester," she said, brightly, "seeing me home from the party."

"Oh!" he yawned.

"Go to sleep."

He fell asleep at once. The stair creaked. The tenement was again quiet....

He was lying in his mother's place in the bed.... She looked out upon the river. Somewhere, far below in the darkness, the current still ran swirling to the sea—where the lights go different ways.... The boy was lying in his mother's place. And before she lifted him, she took his warm little hand, and kissed his brow, where the dark curls lay damp with the sweat of sleep. For a long, long time, she sat watching him through a mist of glad tears. The sight of his face, the outline of his body under the white coverlet, the touch of his warm flesh: all this thrilled her inexpressibly. Had she been devout, she would have thanked God for the gift of a son—and would have found relief.... When she crept in beside him, she drew him to her, tenderly still closer, until he was all contained in her arms; and she forgot all else—and fell asleep, untroubled.

A MEETING BY CHANCE

Came, then, into the lives of these two, to work wide and immediate changes, the Rev. John Fithian, a curate of the Church of the Lifted Cross—a tall, free-moving, delicately spare figure, clad in spotless black, with a hint of fashion about it, a dull gold crucifix lying suspended upon the breast: pale, long of face, the eye-sockets deep and shadowy; hollow-cheeked, the bones high and faintly touched with red; with black, straight, damp hair, brushed back from a smooth brow and falling in the perfection of neatness to the collar— the whole severe and forbidding, indeed, but for saving gray eyes, wherein there lurked, behind the patient agony, often displacing it, a tender smile, benignant, comprehending, infinitely sympathetic, by which the gloomy exterior was lightened and in some surprising way gratefully explained.

By chance, on the first soft spring day of that year, the Rev. John Fithian, returning from the Neighbourhood Settlement, where he had delighted himself with good deeds, done of pure purpose, came near the door of the Box Street tenement, distributing smiles, pennies, impulsive, genuine caresses, to the children as he went, tipping their faces, patting their heads, all in the rare, unquestioned way, being not alien to the manner of the poor. A street piano, at the corner, tinkled an air to which a throng of ragged, lean little girls danced in the yellow sunshine, dodging trucks and idlers and impatient pedestrians with unconcern, colliding and tripping with utmost good nature. The curate was arrested by the voice of a child, singing to the corner accompaniment—low, in the beginning, brooding, tentative, but in a moment rising sure and clear and tender. It was not hard for the Rev. John Fithian to slip a cassock and surplice upon this wistful child, to give him a background of lofty arches and stained windows, to frame the whole in shadows. And, lo! in the chancel of the Church of the Lifted Cross there stood an angel, singing.

The boy looked up, a glance of suspicion, of fear; but he was at once reassured: there was no guile in the smiling gray eyes of the questioner.

"I am waiting," he answered, "for my mother. She will be home soon."

In a swift, penetrating glance, darting far and deep, dwelling briefly, the curate discovered the pathos of the child's life—the unknowing, patient outlook, the vague sense of pain, the bewilderment, the wistful melancholy, the hopeful determination.

"You, too!" he sighed.

The expression of kindred was not comprehended; but the boy was not disquieted by the sigh, by the sudden extinguishment of the beguiling smile.

"She has gone," he continued, "to the wedding of Sir Arthur Coll and Miss Stillison. She will have a very good time."

The curate came to himself with a start and a gasp.

"She's a bridesmaid," the boy added.

"Oh!" ejaculated the curate.

"Why do you say, 'Oh!'" the boy complained, frowning. "Everybody says that," he went on, wistfully; "and I don't know why."

The curate was a gentleman—acute and courteous. "A touch of indigestion," he answered, promptly, laying a white hand on his black waistcoat. "Oh! There it is again!"

"Stomach ache?"

"Well, you might call it that."

The boy was much concerned. "If you come up-stairs," said he, anxiously, "I'll give you some medicine. Mother keeps it for me."

Thus, presently, the curate found himself top-floor rear, in the room that overlooked the broad river, the roofs of the city beyond, the misty hills: upon which the fading sunshine now fell. And having gratefully swallowed the dose, with a broad, persistent smile, he was given a seat by the window, that the beauty of the day, the companionship of the tiny craft on the river, the mystery of the far-off places, might distract and comfort him. From the boy, sitting upright and prim on the extreme edge of a chair, his feet on the rung, his hands on his knees, proceeded a stream of amiable chatter—not the less amiable for being grave—to which the curate, compelled to his best behavior, listened with attention as amiable, as grave: and this concerned the boats, afloat below, the lights on the river, the child's mother, the simple happenings of his secluded life. So untaught was this courtesy, spontaneous, native—so did it spring from natural wish and perception—that the curate was soon more mystified than entertained; and so did the curate's smile increase in gratification and sympathy that the child was presently off the chair, lingering half abashed in the curate's neighbourhood, soon seated familiarly upon his knee, toying with the dull gold crucifix.

"What's this?" he asked.

"It is the symbol," the curate answered, "of the sacrifice of our dear Lord and Saviour."

The Mother

There was no meaning in the words; but the boy held the cross very tenderly, and looked long upon the face of the Man there in torture—and was grieved and awed by the agony....

In the midst of this, the boy's mother entered. She stopped dead beyond the threshold—warned by the unexpected presence to be upon her guard. Her look of amazement changed to a scowl of suspicion. The curate put the boy from his knee. He rose—embarrassed. There was a space of ominous silence.

"What you doing here?" the woman demanded.

"Trespassing."

She was puzzled—by the word, the smile, the quiet voice. The whole was a new, nonplussing experience. Her suspicion was aggravated.

"What you been telling the boy? Eh? What you been saying about me? Hear me? Ain't you got no tongue?" She turned to the frightened child. "Richard," she continued, her voice losing all its quality of anger, "what lies has this man been telling you about your poor mother?"

The boy kept a bewildered silence.

"What you been lying about?" the woman exclaimed, advancing upon the curate, her eyes blazing.

"I have been telling," he answered, still gravely smiling, "the truth."

Her anger was halted—but she was not pacified.

"Telling," the curate repeated, with a little pause, "the truth."

"You been talking about *me*, eh?"

"No; it was of your late husband."

She started.

"I am a curate of the Church of the Lifted Cross," the curate continued, with unruffled composure, "and I have been telling the exact truth concerning— —"

"You been lying!" the woman broke in. "Yes, you have!"

"No—not so," he insisted. "The exact truth concerning the funeral of Dick Slade from the Church of the Lilted Cross. Your son has told me of his father's death—of the funeral, And I have told your son that I distinctly remember the occasion. I have told him, moreover," he added, putting a hand on the boy's shoulder, his eyes faintly twinkling, "that his father was—ah—as I recall him—of most distinguished appearance."

She was completely disarmed.

When, after an agreeable interval, the Rev. John Fithian took his leave, the boy's mother followed him from the room, and closed the door upon the boy. "I'm glad," she faltered, "that you didn't give me away. It was—kind. But I'm sorry you lied—like that. You didn't have to, you know. He's only a child. It's easy to fool him. *You* wouldn't have to lie. But I *got* to lie. It makes him happy—and there's things he mustn't know. He *must* be happy. I can't stand it when he ain't. It hurts me so. But," she added, looking straight into his eyes, gratefully, "you didn't have to lie. And—it was kind." Her eyes fell. "It was—awful kind."

"I may come again?"

She stared at the floor. "Come again?" she muttered. "I don't know."

"I should very much like to come."

"What do you want?" she asked, looking up. "It ain't *me*, is it?"

The curate shook his head.

"Well, what do you want? I thought you was from the Society. I thought you was an agent come to take him away because I wasn't fit to keep him. But it ain't that. And it ain't *me*. What is it you want, anyhow?"

"To come again."

She turned away. He patiently waited. All at once she looked into his eyes, long, deep, intensely—a scrutiny of his very soul.

"You got a good name to keep, ain't you?" she asked.

"Yes," he answered. "And you?"

"It don't matter about me."

"And I may come?"

"Yes," she whispered.

RENUNCIATION

After that the curate came often to the room in the Box Street tenement; but beyond the tenants of top floor rear he did not allow the intimacy to extend—not even to embrace the quaintly love-lorn Mr. Poddle. It was now summer; the window was open to the west wind, blowing in from the sea. Most the curate came at evening, when the breeze was cool and clean, and the lights began to twinkle in the gathering shadows: then to sit at the window, describing unrealities, not conceived in the world of the listeners; and these new and beautiful thoughts, melodiously voiced in the twilight, filled the hours with wonder and strange delight. Sometimes, the boy sang— his mother, too, and the curate: a harmony of tender voices, lifted softly. And once, when the songs were all sung, and the boy had slipped away to the comfort of Mr. Poddle, who was now ill abed with his restless lungs, the curate turned resolutely to the woman.

"I want the boy's voice," he said.

She gave no sign of agitation. "His voice?" she asked, quietly. "Ain't the boy's *self* nothing to your church?"

"Not," he answered, "to the church."

"Not to you?"

"It is very much," he said, gravely, "to me."

"Well?"

He lifted his eyebrows—in amazed comprehension. "I must say, then," he said, bending eagerly towards her, "that I want the boy?"

"The boy," she answered.

For a little while she was silent—vacantly contemplating the bare floor. There had been no revelation. She was not taken unaware. She had watched his purpose form. Long before, she had perceived the issue approaching, and had bravely met it. But it was all now definite and near. She found it hard to command her feeling—bitter to cut the trammels of her love for the child.

"You got to pay, you know," she said, looking up. "Boy sopranos is scarce. You can't have him cheap."

"Of course!" he hastened to say. "The church will pay."

"Money? It ain't money I want."

To this there was nothing to say. The curate was in the dark—and quietly awaited enlightenment.

"Take him!" she burst out, rising. "My God! just you take him. That's all I want. Understand me? I want to get rid of him."

He watched her in amazement. For a time she wandered about the room, distraught, quite aimless: now tragically pausing; now brushing her hand over her eyes—a gesture of weariness and despair. Then she faced him.

"Take him," she said, her voice hoarse. "Take him away from me. I ain't fit to have him. Understand? He's got to grow up into a man. And I can't teach him how. Take him. Take him altogether. Make him—like yourself. Before you come," she proceeded, now feverishly pacing the floor, "I never knew that men was good. No man ever looked in my eyes the way you do. I know them—oh, I know them! And when my boy grows up, I want him to look in the eyes of women the way you look—in mine. Just that! Only that! If only, oh, if only my son will look in the eyes of women the way you look in mine! Understand? I *want* him to. But I can't teach him how. I don't know enough. I ain't good enough."

The curate rose.

"You can't take his voice and leave his soul," she went on. "You got to take his soul. You got to make it—like your own."

"Not like mine!"

"Just," she said, passionately, "like yours. Don't you warn me!" she flashed. "I know the difference between your soul and mine. I know that when his soul is like yours he won't love me no more. But I can't help that. I got to do without him. I got to live my life—and let him live his. It's the way with mothers and sons. God help the mothers! It's the way of the world.... And he'll go with you," she added. "I'll get him so he'll be glad to go. It won't be nice to do—but I can do it. Maybe you think I can't. Maybe you think I love him too much. It ain't that I love him too much. It's because I love him *enough*!"

"You offer the boy to me?"

"Will you take him—voice and soul?"

"I will take him," said the curate, "soul and voice."

She began at once to practice upon the boy's love for her—this skillfully, persistently: without pity for herself or him. She sighed, wept, sat gloomy for hours together: nor would she explain her sorrow, but relentlessly left it to deal with his imagination, by which it was magnified and touched with the horror of mystery. It was not hard—thus to feign sadness, terror, despair: to hint misfortune, parting, unalterable love. Nor could the boy withstand it; by this depression he was soon reduced to a condition of apprehension and grief wherein self-sacrifice was at one with joyful opportunity. Dark days, these—hours of agony, premonition, fearful expectation. And when they had sufficiently wrought upon him, she was ready to proceed.

One night she took him in her lap, in the old close way, in which he loved to be held, and sat rocking, for a time, silently.

"Let us talk, dear," she said.

"I think I'm too sick," he sighed. "I just want to lie here—and not talk."

He had but expressed her own desire—to have him lie there: not to talk, but just to feel him lying in her arms.

"We must," she said.

Something in her voice—something distinguishable from the recent days as deep and real—aroused the boy. He touched the lashes of her eyes—and found them wet.

"Why are you crying?" he asked. "Oh, tell me, mother! Tell me *now!*"

She did not answer.

"I'm sick," he muttered. "I—I—think I'm very sick."

"Something has happened, dear," she said. "I'm going to tell you what." She paused—and in the pause felt his body grow tense in a familiar way. For a moment the prospect frightened her. She felt, vaguely, that she was playing with that which was infinitely delicate—which might break in her very hands, and leave her desolate. "You know, dear," she continued, faltering, "we used to be very rich. But we're not, any more." It was a poor lie—she realized that: and was half ashamed. "We're very poor, now," she went on, hurriedly. "A man broke into the bank and stole all your mother's gold and diamonds and lovely dresses. She hasn't anything—any more." She had conceived a vast contempt for the lie; she felt that it was a weak, unpracticed thing—but she knew that it was sufficient:

45

for he had never yet doubted her. "So I don't know what she'll do," she concluded, weakly. "She will have to stop having good times, I guess. She will have to go to work."

He straightened in her lap. "No, no!" he cried, gladly. "*I'll* work!"

Her impulse was to express her delight in his manliness, her triumphant consciousness of his love—to kiss him, to hug him until he cried out with pain. But she restrained all this—harshly, pitilessly. She had no mercy upon herself.

"I'll work!" he repeated.

"How?" she asked. "You don't know how."

"Teach me."

She laughed—an ironical little laugh: designed to humiliate him. "Why," she exclaimed, "I don't know how to teach you!"

He sighed.

"But," she added, significantly, "the curate knows."

"Then," said he, taking hope, "the curate will teach me."

"Yes; but——"

"But what? Tell me quick, mother!"

"Well," she hesitated, "the curate is so busy. Anyhow, dear," she continued, "I would have to work. We are very poor. You see, dear, it takes a great deal of money to buy new clothes for you. And, then, dear, you see——"

He waited—somewhat disturbed by the sudden failure of her voice. It was all becoming bitter to her, now; she found it hard to continue.

"You see," she gasped, "you eat—quite a bit."

"I'll not eat much," he promised. "And I'll not want new clothes. And it won't take long for the curate to teach me how to work."

She would not agree.

"Tell me!" he commanded.

"Yes," she said; "but the curate says he wants you to live with him."

"Would you come, too?"

"No," she answered.

He did not yet comprehend. "Would I go—alone?"

"Yes."

"All alone?"

"Alone!"

Quiet fell upon all the world—in the twilighted room, in the tenement, in the falling night without, where no breeze moved. The child sought to get closer within his mother's arms, nearer to her bosom—then stirred no more. The lights were flashing into life on the river—wandering aimlessly: but yet drifting to the sea.... Some one stumbled past the door—grumbling maudlin wrath.

"There is no other way," the mother said.

There was no response—a shiver, subsiding at once: no more than that.

"And I would go to see you—quite often."

She tried to see his face; but it was hid against her.

"It would be better," she whispered, "for you."

"Oh, mother," he sobbed, sitting back in her lap, "what would you do without me?"

It was a crucial question—so appealing in unselfish love, so vividly portraying her impending desolation, that for an instant her resolution departed. What would she do without him? God knew! But she commanded herself.

"I would not have to work," she said.

He turned her face to the light—looked deep in her eyes, searching for the truth. She met his glance without wavering. Then, discerning the effect, deliberately, when his eyes were alight with filial love and concern, at the moment when the sacrifice was most clear and most poignant, she lied.

"I would be happier," she said, "without you."

A moan escaped him.

"Will you go with the curate?" she asked.

"Yes."

He fell back upon her bosom....

There was no delay. 'Twas all done in haste. The night came. Gently the curate took the child from her arms.

"Good-bye," she said.

"I said I would not cry, mother," he faltered. "I am not crying."

"Good-bye, dear."

"Mother, I am not crying."

"You are very brave," she said, discovering his wish. "Good-bye. Be a good boy."

He took the curate's hand. They moved to the door—but there turned and lingered. While the child looked upon his mother, bravely calling a smile to his face, that she might be comforted, there crept into his eyes, against his will, some reproach. Perceiving this, she staggered towards him, but halted at the table, which she clutched: and there stood, her head hanging forward, her body swaying. Then she levelled a finger at the curate.

"Take him away, you damn fool!" she screamed.

IN THE CURRENT

Seven o'clock struck. It made no impression upon her. Eight o'clock—nine o'clock. It was now dark. Ten o'clock. She did not hear. Still at the window, her elbow on the sill, her chin resting in her hand, she kept watch on the river—but did not see the river: but saw the sea, wind-tossed and dark, where the lights go wide apart. Eleven o'clock. Ghostly moonlight filled the room. The tenement, restless in the summer heat, now sighed and fell asleep. Twelve o'clock. She had not moved: nor dared she move. There was a knock at the door—a quick step behind her. She turned in alarm.

"Millie!"

She rose. Voice and figure were well known to her. She started forward—but stopped dead.

"Is it you, Jim?" she faltered.

"Yes, Millie. It's me—come back. You don't feel the way you did before, do you, girl?" He suddenly subdued his voice—as though recollecting a caution. "You ain't going to send me away, are you?" he asked.

"Go 'way!" she complained. "Leave me alone."

He came nearer.

"Give me a show, Jim," she begged. "Go 'way. It ain't fair to come—now. Hear me?" she cried, in protest against his nearer approach, her voice rising shrilly. "It ain't fair——"

"Hist!" he interrupted. "You'll wake the——"

She laughed harshly. "Wake what?" she mocked. "Eh, Jim? What'll I wake?"

"Why, Millie!" he exclaimed. "You'll wake the boy."

"Boy!" she laughed. "What boy? There ain't no boy. Look here!" she cried, rushing impetuously to the bed, throwing back the coverlet, wildly tossing the pillows to the floor. "What'll I wake? Eh, Jim? Where's the boy I'll wake?" She turned upon him. "What you saying 'Hist!' for? Hist!" she mocked, with a laugh. "Talk as loud as you like, Jim. You don't need to care what you say or how you say it. There ain't nobody here to mind you. For I tell you," she stormed, "there ain't no boy—no more!"

He caught her hand.

"Let go my hand!" she commanded. "Keep off, Jim! I ain't in no temper to stand it—to-night."

He withdrew. "Millie," he asked, in distress, "the boy ain't——"

"Dead?" she laughed. "No. I give him away. He was different from us. I didn't have no right to keep him. I give him to a parson. Because," she added, defiantly, "I wasn't fit to bring him up. And he ain't here no more," she sighed, blankly sweeping the moonlit room. "I'm all alone—now."

"Poor girl!" he muttered.

She was tempted by this sympathy. "Go home, Jim," she said. "It ain't fair to stay. I'm all alone, now—and it ain't treating me right."

"Millie," he answered, "you ain't treating yourself right."

She flung out her arms—in dissent and hopelessness.

"No, you ain't," he continued. "You've give him up. You're all alone. You can't go on—alone. Millie, girl," he pleaded, softly, "I want you. Come to me!"

She wavered.

"Come to me!" he repeated, his voice tremulous, his arms extended. "You're all alone. You've lost him. Come to me!"

"Lost him?" she mused. "No—not that. If I'd lost him, Jim, I'd take you. If ever he looked in my eyes—as if I'd lost him—I'd take you. I've give him up; but I ain't lost him. Maybe," she proceeded, eagerly, "when the time comes, he'll not give me up. He loves me, Jim; he'll not forget. I know he's different from us. You can't tell a mother nothing about such things as that. God!" she muttered, clasping her hands, "how strangely different he is. And every day he'll change. Every day he'll be—more different. That's what I want. That's why I give him up. To make him—more different! But maybe," she continued, her voice rising with the intensity of her feeling, "when he grows up, and the time comes—maybe, Jim, when he can't be made no more different—maybe, when I go to him, man grown—are you listening?—maybe, when I ask him if he loves me, he'll remember! Maybe, he'll take me in. Lost him?" she asked. "How do you know that? Go to you, Jim? Go to you, now—when he might take me in if I wait? I can't! Don't you understand? When the time comes, he might ask me—where you was."

"You're crazy, Millie," the man protested. "You're just plain crazy."

"Crazy? Maybe, I am. To love and hope! Crazy? Maybe, I am. But, Jim, mothers is all that way."

"All that way?" he asked, regarding her with a speculative eye.

"Mothers," she repeated, "is all that way."

"Well," said he, swiftly advancing, "lovers isn't."

"Keep back!" she cried.

"No, I won't."

"You'll make a cat of me. I warn you, Jim!"

"You can't keep me off. You said you loved me. You do love me. You can't help yourself. You got to marry me."

She retreated. "Leave me alone!" she screamed. "I can't. Don't you see how it is? Quit that, now, Jim! You ain't fair. Take your arms away. God help me! I love you, you great big brute! You know I do. You ain't fair.... Stop! You hurt me." She was now in his arms—but still resisting. "Leave me alone," she whimpered. "You hurt me. You ain't fair. You know I love you—and you ain't fair.... Oh, God forgive me! Don't do that again, Jim. Stop! Let me go. For God's sake, stop kissing me! I like you, Jim. I ain't denying that. But let me go.... Please, Jim! Don't hold me so tight. It ain't fair.... Oh, it ain't fair...."

She sank against his broad breast; and there she lay helpless— bitterly sobbing.

"Don't cry, Millie!" he whispered.

Still she sobbed.

"Oh, don't cry, girl!" he repeated, tenderly. "It's all right. I won't hurt you. You love me, and I love you. That's all right, Millie. What's the matter with you, girl? Lift your face, won't you?"

"No, no!"

"Why not, Millie?"

"I don't know," she whispered. "I think I'm—ashamed."

There was no longer need to hold her fast. His arms relaxed. She did not move from them. And while they stood thus, in the moonlight, falling brightly through the window, he stroked her hair, murmuring, the while, all the reassuring words at his command.

"The boy's gone," he said, at last. "You'd be all alone without me. He ain't here. But he's well looked after, Millie. Don't you fret about him. By this time he's sound asleep."

She slipped from his embrace. He made no effort to detain her: conceiving her secure in his possession. A moment she stood staring at the floor, lost to her surroundings: then quickly turned to look upon him—her face aglow with some high tenderness.

"Asleep?" she asked, her voice low, tremulous.

"Sound asleep."

"How do you know that he's asleep?" she pursued. "Asleep? No; he ain't asleep." She paused—now woebegone. "He's wide awake— waiting," she went on. "He's waiting—just like he used to do—for me to come in.... He's awake. Oh, sore little heart! He's lying alone in the dark—waiting. And his mother will not come.... Last night, Jim, when I come in, he was there in the bed, awake and waiting. 'Oh, mother,' says he, 'I'm glad you're come at last. I been waiting so long. It's lonesome here in the dark without you. And to-morrow I'll wake, and wait, and wait; but you will not come!' He's awake, Jim. Don't you tell me no different. The pillow's wet with his tears.... Lonely child—waiting for me! Oh, little heart of my baby! Oh, sore little heart!"

"Millie!"

"It ain't no use no more, Jim. You better go home. I'm all alone. My child's not here. But—he's somewhere. And it's him I love."

The Mother

The man sighed and went away....

Left alone, she put the little room in order and made the bed, blinded by tears, her steps uncertain: muttering incoherently of her child, whimpering broken snatches of lullaby songs. When there was no more work left for her hands to do, she staggered to the bureau, and from the lower drawer took a great, flaunting doll, which she had there kept, poor soul! against the time when her arms would be empty, her bosom aching for a familiar weight upon it. And for a time she sat rocking the cold counterfeit, crooning, faintly singing, caressing it; but she had known the warmth, the sweet restlessness, the soft, yielding form of the living child, and could not be content. Presently, in a surge of disgust, she flung the substitute violently from her.

"It ain't no baby," she moaned, putting her hands to her face. "It's only a doll!"

She sank limp to the floor. There she lay prone—the moonlight falling softly upon her, but healing her not at all.

THE CHORISTER

The Rev. John Fithian lived alone with a man-servant in a wide-windowed, sombre, red old house, elbowed by tenements, near the Church of the Lifted Cross—once a fashionable quarter: now mean, dejected, incongruously thronged, and fast losing the last appearances of respectability. Sombre without—half-lit, silent, vast within: the whole intolerant of frivolity, inharmony, garishness, ugliness, but yet quite free of gloom and ghostly suggestion. The boy tiptoed over the thick carpets, spoke in whispers, eyed the shadowy corners—sensitive to impressions, forever alert: nevertheless possessing a fine feeling of security and hopefulness; still wistful, often weeping in the night, but not melancholy. Responsive to environment, by nature harmonious with his new surroundings, he presently moved through the lofty old rooms with a manner reflecting their own—the same gravity, serenity, old-fashioned grace: expressing even their stateliness in a quaint and childish way. Thus was the soil of his heart prepared for the seed of a great change.

By and by the curate enlightened the child concerning sin and the Vicarious Sacrifice. This was when the leaves were falling from the trees in the park—a drear, dark night: the wind sweeping the streets in violent gusts, the rain lashing the windowpanes. Night had come unnoticed—swiftly, intensely: in the curate's study a change from gray twilight to firelit shadows. The boy was squatted on the hearth-rug, disquieted by the malicious beating at the window, glad to be in the glow of the fire: his visions all of ragged men and women cowering from the weather.

The Mother

"It is time, now," the curate sighed, "that I told you the story."

"What story?"

"The story of the Man who died for us."

The boy turned—in wonderment. "I did not know," he said, quickly, "that a man had died for us. What was his name? Why did he do it? My mother never told me that story."

"I think she does not know it."

"Then I'll tell her when I learn."

"Perhaps," said the curate, "she will like to hear it—from you."

Very gently, then, in his deep, mellifluous voice—while the rain beat upon the windows, crying out the sorrows of the poor—the curate unfolded the poignant story: the terms simple, the recital clear, vivid, complete.... And to the heart of this child the appeal was immediate and irresistible.

"And they who sin," the curate concluded, "crucify Him again."

"I love that Jesus!" the boy sobbed. "I love Him—almost as much as mother."

"Almost?"

The boy misunderstood. He felt reproved. He flushed—ashamed that the new love had menaced the old. "No," he answered; "but I love Him very much."

"Not as much?"

"Oh, I could not!"

The boy was never afterwards the same. All that was inharmonious in life—the pain and poverty and unloveliness—became as sin: a continuous crucifixion, hateful, wringing the heart....

Late in the night, when he lay sleepless, sick for his mother's presence, her voice, her kisses, her soothing touch, the boy would rise to sit at the window—there to watch shadowy figures flit through the street-lamp's circle of light. Once he fancied that his mother came thus out of the night, that for a moment she paused with upturned glance, then disappeared in woe and haste: returning, halted again; but came no more....

At rare intervals the boy's mother came to the curate's door. She would not enter: but timidly waited for her son, and then went with him to the park, relieved to be away from the wide, still house, her spirits and self-confidence reviving with every step. One mellow evening, while they sat together in the dusk, an ill-clad man, gray and unkempt, shuffled near.

"Mother," the boy whispered, gripping her hand, "he is looking at us."

She laughed. "Let him look!" said she. "It don't matter."

The man staggered to the bench—heavily sat down: limp and shameless, his head hanging.

"Let us go away!" the boy pleaded.

"Why, darling?" his mother asked, puzzled. "What's the matter with you, anyhow?" She looked at him—realizing some subtle change in him, bewildered by it: searching eagerly for the nature and cause. "You didn't used to be like that," she said.

"I don't like him. He's wicked. He frightens me."

The man slipped suddenly from the bench—sprawling upon the walk. The woman laughed.

"Don't laugh!" the boy exclaimed—a cry of reproach, not free of indignation. "Oh, mother," he complained, putting her hand to his cheek, "how could you!"

She did not answer. The derelict picked himself up, whining in a maudlin way.

"How could you!" the boy repeated.

"Oh," said she, lightly, "he's all right. He won't hurt us."

"He's wicked!"

"He's drunk. It don't matter. What's come over you, dear?"

"I'm afraid," said the boy. "He's sinful."

"He's only drunk, poor man!"

High over the houses beyond, the steeple of the Church of the Lifted Cross pierced the blue-black sky. It was tipped with a blazing cross—a great cross, flaming in the night: a symbol of sacrifice, a hope, a protest, raised above the feverish world. To this the boy looked. It transported him far from the woman whose hand he clutched.

"They who sin," he muttered, his eyes still turned to the lifted cross, "crucify the dear Lord again!"

His mother was both mystified and appalled. She followed his glance—but saw only the familiar landmark: an illuminated cross, topping a steeple.

"For God's sake, Richard!" she demanded, "what you talking about?"

He did not hear.

"You ain't sick, are you?" she continued.

He shook his head.

"What's the matter with you?" she implored. "Oh, tell your mother!"

He loosened his hand from her clasp, withdrew it: but instantly caught her hand again, and kissed it passionately. So much concerned was she for his physical health that the momentary shrinking escaped her.

"You're sick," she said. "I know you are. You're singing too much in the church."

"No."

"Then you're eating too much lemon pie," she declared, anxiously. "You're too fond of that. It upsets your stomach. Oh, Richard! Shame, dear! I told you not to."

"You told me not to eat *much*," he said. "So I don't eat any — to make sure."

She was aware of the significance of this sacrifice — and kissed him quickly in fond approval. Then she turned up his coat-sleeve. "The fool!" she cried. "You got cold. That's what's the matter with you. Here it is November! And he ain't put your flannels on. That there curate," she concluded, in disgust, "don't know nothing about raising a boy."

"I'm quite well, mother."

"Then what's the matter with you?"

"I'm sad!" he whispered.

She caught him to her breast — blindly misconceiving the meaning of this: in her ignorance concluding that he longed for her, and was sick because of that.... And while she held him close, the clock of the Church of the Lifted Cross chimed seven. In haste she put him down, kissed him, set him on his homeward way; and she watched him until he was lost in the dusk and distance of the park. Then, concerned, bewildered, she made haste to that quarter of the city — that swarming, flaring, blatant place — where lay her occupation for the night.

Near Christmas, in a burst of snowy weather, the boy sang his first solo at the Church of the Lifted Cross: this at evening. His mother, conspicuously gowned, somewhat overcome by the fashion of the place, which she had striven to imitate — momentarily chagrined by her inexplicable failure to be in harmony — seated herself obscurely, where she had but an infrequent glimpse of his white robe, wistful face, dark, curling hair. She had never loved him more proudly — never before realized that his value extended beyond the region of her arms: never before known that the babe, the child, the growing boy, mothered by her, nursed at her breast, her possession, was a gift to the world, sweet and inspiring. "Angels, ever bright and fair!" She felt the thrill of his tender voice; perceived the impression: the buzz, the subsiding confusion, the spell-bound stillness. "Take, oh, take me to your care!" It was in her heart to strike her breasts — to cry out that this was her son, born of her; her bosom his place....

When the departing throng had thinned in the aisle, she stepped from the pew, and stood waiting. There passed, then, a lady in rich attire — sweet-faced, of exquisite manner. A bluff, ruddy young man attended her.

"Did you like the music?" he asked — a conventional question: everywhere repeated.

"Perfectly lovely!" she replied. "A wonderful voice! And such a pretty child!"

"I wonder," said he, "who the boy can be?"

Acting upon ingenuous impulse, the boy's mother overtook the man, timidly touched his elbow, looked into his eyes, her own bright with proud love.

"He is my son," she said.

The lady turned in amazement. In a brief, appraising glance, she comprehended the whole woman; the outré gown, the pencilled eyebrows, the rouged cheeks, the bleached hair. She took the man's arm.

"Come!" she said.

The man yielded. He bowed—smiled in an embarrassed way, flushing to his sandy hair: turned his back.

"How strange!" the lady whispered.

The woman was left alone in the aisle—not chagrined by the rebuff, being used to this attitude, sensitive no longer: but now knowing, for the first time, that the world into which her child had gone would not accept her.... The church was empty. The organ had ceased. One by one the twinkling lights were going out. The boy came bounding down the aisle. With a glad little cry he leaped into her waiting arms....

ALIENATION

This night, after a week of impatient expectation, they were by the curate's permission to spend together in the Box Street tenement. It was the boy's first return to the little room overlooking the river. Thither they hurried through the driving snow, leaning to the blasts, unconscious of the bitterness of the night: the twain in high spirits — the boy chattering, merrily, incoherently, as he trotted at his silent mother's side. Very happy, now, indeed, they raced up the stair, rioting up flight after flight, to top floor rear, where there was a cheery fire, a kettle bubbling on the stove, a lamp turned low — a feeling of warmth and repose and welcome, which the broad window, noisily shaken by a hearty winter wind from the sea, pleasantly accentuated.

The gladness of this return, the sudden, overwhelming realization of a longing that had been agonizing in its intensity, excited the boy beyond bounds. He gave an indubitable whoop of joy, which so startled and amazed the woman that she stared open-mouthed; tossed his cap in the air, flung his overcoat and gloves on the floor, peeped through the black window-panes, pried into the cupboard, hugged his mother so rapturously, so embarrassingly, that he tumbled her over and was himself involved in the hilarious collapse: whereupon, as a measure of protection while she laid the table, she despatched him across the hall to greet Mr. Poddle, who was ill abed, anxiously awaiting him.

The Dog-faced Man was all prinked for the occasion — his hirsute adornment neatly brushed and braided, smoothly parted from crown over brow and nose to chin: so that, though, to be sure, his appearance instantly suggested a porcupine, his sensitive lips and mild gray eyes were for once allowed to impress the beholder. The air of Hockley's Musee had at last laid him by the heels. No longer, by any license of metaphor, could his lungs be said to be merely restless. He was flat on his back—white, wan, gasping: sweat dampening the hair on his brow. But he bravely chirked up when the child entered, subdued and pitiful; and though, in response to a glance of pain and concern, his eyes overran with the weak tears of the sick, he smiled like a man to whom Nature had not been cruel, while he pressed the small hand so swiftly extended.

"I'm sick, Richard," he whispered. "'Death No Respecter of Persons.' Git me? 'High and Low Took By the Grim Reaper.' I'm awful sick."

The boy, now seated on the bed, still holding the ghastly hand, hoped that Mr. Poddle would soon be well.

"No," said the Dog-faced Man. "I won't. 'Climax of a Notable Career.' Git me? It wouldn't—be proper."

Not proper?

"No, Richard. It really wouldn't be proper. 'Dignified in Death.' Understand? Distinguished men has their limits. 'Outlived His Fame.' I really couldn't stand it. Git me?"

"Not—quite."

"Guess I'll have to tell you. Look!" The Dog-faced Man held up his hand—but swiftly replaced it between the child's warm, sympathetic palms. "No rings. Understand? 'Pawned the Family Jewells.' Git me? 'Reduced to Poverty.' Where's my frock coat? Where's my silk hat? 'Wardrobe of a Celebrity Sold For A Song.' Where's them two pair of trousers? 'A Tragic Disappearance.' All up the spout. Everything gone. 'Not a Stitch to His Name.' Really, Richard, it wouldn't be proper to get well. A natural phenomenon of my standing couldn't— simply *couldn't*, Richard—go back to the profession with a wardrobe consistin' of two pink night-shirts, both the worse for wear. It wouldn't *do*! On the Stage In Scant Attire.' I couldn't stand it. 'Fell From His High Estate.' It would break my heart."

No word of comfort occurred to the boy.

"So," sighed the Dog-faced Man, "I guess I better die. And the quicker the better."

To change the distressful drift of the conversation, the boy inquired concerning the Mexican Sword Swallower.

"Hush!" implored Mr. Poddle, in a way so poignant that the boy wished he had been more discreet. "Them massive proportions! Them socks! 'Her Fate a Tattooed Man,'" he pursued, in gentle melancholy. "Don't ask me! 'Nearing the Fateful Hour.' Poor child!' Wedded To A Artificial Freak.'"

"Is she married?"

"No—not yet," Mr. Poddle explained. "But when the dragon's tail is finished, accordin' to undenigeable report, the deed will be did. 'Shackled For Life.' Oh, my God! He's borrowed the money to pay the last installment; and I'm informed that only the scales has to be picked out with red. But why should I mourn?" he asked. "'Adored From Afar.' Understand? That's what I got to do. 'His Love a Tragedy.' Oh, Richard," Mr. Poddle concluded, in genuine distress, "that's me! It couldn't be nothing else. Natural phenomens is natural phenomens. 'Paid the Penalty of Genius.' That's me!"

The boy's mother called to him.

"Richard," said Mr. Poddle, abruptly, "I'm awful sick. I can't last much longer. Git me? I'm dyin'. And I'm poor. I ain't got a cent. I'm forgot by the public. I'm all alone in the world. Nobody owes me no kindness." He clutched the boy's hand. "Know who pays my rent? Know who feeds me? Know who brings the doctor when I vomit blood? Know who sits with me in the night—when I can't sleep?

Know who watches over me? Who comforts me? Who holds my hand when I git afraid to die? Know who that is, Richard?"

"Yes," the boy whispered.

"Who is it?"

"My mother!"

"Yes—your mother," said the Dog-faced Man. He lifted himself on the pillow. "Richard," he continued, "listen to me! I'll be dead, soon, and then I can't talk to you no more. I can't say no word to you from the grave—when the time she dreads has come. Listen to me!" His voice rose. He was breathing in gasps. There was a light in his eyes. "It is your mother. There ain't a better woman in all the world. Listen to me! Don't you forget her. She loves you. You're all she's got. Her poor heart is hungry for you. Don't you forget her. There ain't a better woman nowhere. There ain't a woman more fit for heaven. Don't you go back on her! Don't you let no black-and-white curick teach you no different!"

"I'll not forget!" said the boy.

Mr. Poddle laid a hand on his head. "God bless you, Richard!" said he.

The boy kissed him, unafraid of his monstrous countenance—and then fled to his mother....

For a long time the Dog-faced Man lay alone, listening to the voices across the hall: himself smiling to know that the woman had her son again; not selfishly reluctant to be thus abandoned. The door was ajar. Joyous sounds drifted in—chatter, soft laughter, the rattle of dishes.... Presently, silence: broken by the creaking of the rocking-chair, and by low singing.... By and by, voices, speaking gravely—in intimate converse: this for a long, long time, while the muttering of the tenement ceased, and quiet fell.... A plea and an imploring protest. She was wanting him to go to bed. There followed the familiar indications that the child was being disrobed: shoes striking the floor, yawns, sleepy talk, crooning encouragement.... Then a strange silence—puzzling to the listener: not accountable by his recollection of similar occasions.

There was a quick step in the hall.

"Poddle!"

The Dog-faced Man started. There was alarm in the voice—despair, resentment. On the threshold stood the woman—distraught: one hand against the door-post, the other on her heart.

"Poddle, he's——"

Mr. Poddle, thrown into a paroxysm of fright by the pause, struggled to his elbow, but fell back, gasping.

"What's he doin'?" he managed to whisper.

"Prayin'!" she answered, hoarsely.

Mr. Poddle was utterly nonplussed. The situation was unprecedented: not to be dealt with on the basis of past experience.

"'Religion In Haste,'" he sighed, sadly confounded. "'Repent At Leisure.'"

"Prayin'!" she repeated, entering on tiptoe. "He's down on his knees—*prayin'*!" She began to pace the floor—wringing her hands: a tragic figure. "It's come, Poddle!" she whimpered, beginning now to bite at her fingernails. "He's changed. He never seen me pray. *I* never told him how. Oh, he's—different. And he'll change more. I got to face it. He'll soon be like the people that—that—don't understand us. I couldn't stand it to see that stare in his eyes. It'll kill me, Poddle! I knew it would come," she continued, uninterrupted, Mr. Poddle being unable to come to her assistance for lack of breath. "But I didn't think it would be so—awful soon. And I didn't know

67

how much it would hurt. I didn't *think* about it. I didn't dare. Oh, my baby!" she sobbed. "You'll not love your mother any more—when you find her out. You'll be just like—all them people!" She came to a full stop. "Poddle," she declared, trembling, her voice rising harshly, "I got to do something. I got to do it—*quick*! What shall I do? Oh, what shall I do?"

Mr. Poddle drew a long breath. "Likewise!" he gasped.

She did not understand.

"Likewise!" Mr. Poddle repeated. "'Fought the Devil With Fire.' Quick!" He weakly beckoned her to be off. "Don't—let him know—you're different. Go and—pray yourself. Don't—let on you—never done it—before."

She gave him a glad glance of comprehension—and disappeared...

The boy had risen.

"Oh!" she exclaimed, brightly. "You got through, didn't you, dear?"

He was now sitting on the edge of the bed, his legs dangling—still reluctant to crawl within. And he was very gravely regarding her, a cloud of anxious wonder in his eyes.

"Who taught you to," she hesitated, "do it—that way?" she pursued, making believe to be but lightly interested. "The curate? Oh, my!" she exclaimed, immediately changing the thought. "Your mother's awful sleepy." She counterfeited a yawn. "I never kneel to—do it," she continued. In a sharp glance she saw the wonder clearing from his eyes, the beginnings of a smile appear about his lips; and she was emboldened to proceed. "Some kneels," she said, "and some doesn't. The curate, I suppose, kneels. That's his way. Now, *I* don't. I was brought up—the other way. I wait till I get in bed to—say mine. When you was a baby," she rattled, "I used to—keep it up—for hours at a time. I just *love* to—do it. In bed, you know. I guess you never seen me kneel, did you? But I think I will, after this, because you—do it—that way."

His serenity was quite restored. Glad to learn that his mother knew the solace of prayer, he rolled back on the pillows. She tucked him in.

"Now, watch me," she said.

"And I," said he, "will pray all over again. In bed," he added; "because that's the way *you* do it."

She knelt. "In God's name!" she thought, as she inclined her bead, "what can I do? I've lost him. Oh, I've lost him.... What'll I do when he finds out? He'll not love me then. Love me!" she thought, bitterly. "He'll look at me like them people in the church. I can't stand it! I got to *do* something.... It won't be long. They'll tell him—some one. And I can't do nothing to help it! But I *got* to do something.... My God! I got to do something. I'll dress better than this. This foulard's a botch." New fashions in dress, in coiffures, multiplied in her mind. She was groping, according to her poor enlightenment. "The pompadour!" she mused, inspired, according to the inspiration of her kind. "It might suit my style. I'll try it.... But, oh, it won't do no good," she thought, despairing. "*It* won't do no good.... I've lost him! Good God! I've lost my own child...."

She rose.

"It took you an awful long time," said the boy.

"Yes," she answered, absently. "I'm the real thing. When I pray, I pray good and hard."

A CHILD'S PRAYER

The boy's room was furnished in the manner of the curate's chamber—which, indeed, was severe and chaste enough: for the curate practiced certain monkish austerities not common to the clergy of this day. It was a white, bare little room, at the top of the house, overlooking the street: a still place, into which, at bedtime, no distraction entered to break the nervous introspection, the high, wistful dreaming, sadly habitual to the child when left alone in the dark. But always, of fine mornings, the sun came joyously to waken him; and often, in the night, when he lay wakeful, the moon peeped in upon the exquisite simplicity, and, discovering a lonely child, companionably lingered to hearten him. The beam fell over the window-sill, crawled across the floor, climbed the bare wall.

There was a great white crucifix on the wall, hanging in the broad path of the moonlight. It stared at the boy's pillow, tenderly appealing: the head thorn-crowned, the body drawn tense, the face uplifted in patient agony. Sometimes it made the boy cry.

"They who sin," he would repeat, "crucify the dear Lord again!"

It would be very hard, then, to fall asleep....

So did the crucifix on the wall work within the child's heart—so did the shadows of the wide, still house impress him, so did the curate's voice and gentle teaching, so did the gloom, the stained windows, the lofty arches, the lights and low, sweet music of the Church of the Lifted Cross favour the subtle change—that he was now moved to pain and sickening disgust by rags and pinched faces and discord and dirt and feverish haste and all manner of harshness and unloveliness, conceiving them poignant as sin....

Mother and son were in the park. It was evening—dusk: a grateful balm abroad in the air. Men and women, returning from church, idled through the spring night.

"But, dear," said his mother, while she patted his hand, "you mustn't *hate* the wicked!"

He looked up in wonder.

"Oh, my! no," she pursued. "Poor things! They're not so bad—when you know them. Some is real kind."

"I could not *love* them!"

"Why not?"

"I *could* not!"

So positive, this—the suggestion so scouted—that she took thought for her own fate.

"Would you love me?" she asked.

"Oh, mother!" he laughed.

"What would you do," she gravely continued, "if I was—a wicked woman?"

He laughed again.

"What would you do," she insisted, "if somebody told you I was bad?"

"Mother," he answered, not yet affected by her earnestness, "you could not be!"

She put her hands on his shoulders. "What would you do?" she repeated.

"Don't!" he pleaded, disquieted.

Again the question—low, intense, demanding answer. He trembled. She was not in play. A sinful woman? For a moment he conceived the possibility—vaguely: in a mere flash of feeling.

"What would you do?"

"I don't know!"

She sighed.

"I think," he whispered, "that I'd—die!"

That night, when the moonlight had climbed to the crucifix on the wall, the boy got out of bed. For a long time he stood in the beam of soft light—staring at the tortured Figure.

"I think I'd better do it!" he determined.

He knelt—lifted his clasped hands—began his childish appeal.

"Dear Jesus," he prayed, "my mother says that I must not hate the wicked. You heard her, didn't you, dear Jesus? It was in the park, to-night, after church—at the bench near the lilac bush. You *must* have heard her.... Mother says the wicked are kind, and not so bad. I would like very much to love them. She says they're nice—when you know them. I know she's right, of course. But it seems queer. And she says I *ought* to love them. So I want to do it, if you don't mind.... Maybe, if you would let me be a little wicked for a little while, I could do it. Don't you think, Jesus, dear, that it is a good idea? A little wicked—for just a little while. I wouldn't care very much, if you didn't mind. But if it hurts you very much, I don't want to, if you please.... But I would like to be a little wicked. If I do, please don't forget me. I would not like to be wicked long. Just a little while. Then I would be good again—and love the wicked, as my mother wants me to do. Good-bye. I mean—Amen!"

The child knew nothing about sin.

MR. PODDLE'S FINALE

Of a yellow, balmy morning, with a languid breeze stirring the curtains in the open windows of the street, a hansom cab, drawn by a lean gray beast, appeared near the curate's door. What with his wild career, the nature of his errand, the extraordinary character of his fare, the driver was all elbows and eyes—a perspiring, gesticulating figure, swaying widely on the high perch.

Within was a lady so monstrously stout that she completely filled the vehicle. Rolls of fat were tucked into every nook, jammed into every corner, calked into every crevice; and, at last, demanding place, they scandalously overflowed the apron. So tight was the fit—so crushed and confined the lady's immensity—that, being quite unable to articulate or stir, but desiring most heartily to do both, she could do little but wheeze, and faintly wave a gigantic hand.

Proceeding thus—while the passenger gasped, and the driver gesticulated, and the hansom creaked and tottered, and the outraged horse bent to the fearful labour—the equipage presently arrived at the curate's door, and was there drawn up with a jerk.

The Fat Lady was released, assisted to alight, helped across the pavement; and having waddled up three steps of the flight, and being unable without a respite to lift her massive foot for the fourth time, she loudly demanded of the impassive door the instant appearance of Dickie Slade: whereupon, the door flew open, and the boy bounded out.

"Madame Lacara!" he cried.

"Quick, child!" the Fat Lady wheezed. "Git your hat. Your mother can't stay no longer—and I can't get up the stairs—and Poddle's dyin'—and *git your hat!*"

In a moment the boy returned. The Fat Lady was standing beside the cab—the exhausted horse contemplating her with no friendly eye.

"Git in!" said she.

"Don't you do it," the driver warned.

"Git in!" the Fat Lady repeated.

"Not if he knows what's good for him," said the driver. "Not first."

The boy hesitated.

"Git in, child!" screamed the Fat Lady.

"Don't you do it," said the driver.

"Child," the Fat Lady gasped, exasperated, "git in!"

"Not first," the driver repeated. "There ain't room for both; and once she lets her weight down——"

"Maybe," the Fat Lady admitted, after giving the matter most careful consideration, "it would be better for you to set on me."

"Maybe," the boy agreed, much relieved, "it would."

So Madame Lacara entered, and took the boy in her arms; and off, at last, they went towards the Box Street tenement, swaying, creaking, wheezing, with a troop of joyous urchins in the wake....

The Mother

It was early afternoon—with the sunlight lying thick and warm on the window-ledge of Mr. Poddle's room, about to enter, to distribute cheer, to speak its unfailing promises. The sash was lifted high; a gentle wind, clean and blue, blowing from the sea, over the roofs and the river, came sportively in, with a joyous little rush and swirl—but of a sudden failed: hushed, as though by unexpected encounter with the solemnity within.

The boy's mother was gone. It was of a Saturday; she had not dared to linger. When the boy entered, Mr. Poddle lay alone, lifted on the pillows, staring deep into the wide, shining sky: composed and dreamful. The distress of his deformity, as the pains of dissolution, had been mitigated by the woman's kind and knowing hand: the tawny hair, by nature rank and shaggy, by habit unkempt, now damp with sweat, was everywhere laid smooth upon his face— brushed away from the eyes: no longer permitted to obscure the fast failing sight.

Beside him, close—drawing closer—the boy seated himself. Very low and broken—husky, halting—was the Dog-faced Man's voice. The boy must often bend his ear to understand.

"The hirsute," Mr. Poddle whispered, "adornment. All ready for the last appearance. 'Natural Phenomonen Meets the Common Fate.' Celebrities," he added, with a little smile, "is just clay."

The boy took his hand.

"She done it," Mr. Poddle explained, faintly indicating the unusual condition of his deforming hair, "with a little brush."

"She?" the boy asked, with significant emphasis.

"No," Mr. Poddle sighed. "Hush! Not She—just her."

By this the boy knew that the Mexican Sword Swallower had not relented—but that his mother had been kind.

"She left that there little brush somewheres," Mr. Poddle continued, with an effort to lift his head, but failing to do more than roll his glazed eyes. "There was a little handkerchief with it. Can't you find 'em, Richard? I wish you could. They make me—more comfortable. Oh, I'm glad you got 'em! I feel easier—this way. She said you'd stay with me—to the last. She said, Richard, that maybe you'd keep the hair away from my eyes, and the sweat from rollin' in. For I'm easier that way; and I want to *see*," he moaned, "to the last!"

The boy pressed his hand.

"I'm tired of the hair," Mr. Poddle sighed. "I used to be proud of it; but I'm tired of it—now. It's been admired, Richard; it's been applauded. Locks of it has been requested by the Fair; and the Strong has wished they was me. But, Richard, celebrities sits on a lonely eminence. And I *been* lonely, God knows! though I kept a smilin' face.... I'm tired of the hair—tired of fame. It all looks different—when you git sight of the Common Leveller. 'Tired of His Talent.' Since I been lyin' here, Richard, sick and alone, I been thinkin' that talent wasn't nothin' much after all. I been wishin', Richard—wishin'!"

The Dog-faced Man paused for breath.

"I been wishin'," he gasped, "that I wasn't a phenomonen—but only a man!"

The sunlight began to creep towards Mr. Poddle's bed—a broad, yellow beam, stretching into the blue spaces without: lying like a golden pathway before him.

"Richard," said Mr. Poddle, "I'm goin' to die."

The boy began to cry.

"Don't cry!" Mr. Poddle pleaded. "I ain't afraid. Hear me, Richard? I ain't afraid."

"No, no!"

"I'm glad to die. 'Death the Dog-faced Man's Best Friend.' I'm glad! Lyin' here, I seen the truth. It's only when a man looks back that he finds out what he's missed—only when he looks back, from the end of the path, that he sees the flowers he might have plucked by the way.... Lyin' here, I been lookin' back—far back. And my eyes is opened. Now I see—now I know! I have been travellin' a road where the flowers grows thick. But God made me so I couldn't pick 'em. It's love, Richard, that men wants. Just love! It's love their hearts is thirsty for.... And there wasn't no love—for me. I been awful thirsty, Richard; but there wasn't no water anywhere in all the world—for me. 'Spoiled In the Making.' That's me. 'God's Bad Break.' Oh, that's me! I'm not a natural phenomonen no more. I'm only a freak of nature. I ain't got no kick comin'. I stand by what God done. Maybe it wasn't no mistake; maybe He wanted to show all the people in the world what would happen if He was in the habit of gittin' careless. Anyhow, I guess He's man enough to stand by the job He done. He made me what I am—a freak. I ain't to blame. But, oh, my God! Richard, it hurts—to be that!"

The boy brushed the tears from the Dog-faced Man's eyes.

"No," Mr. Poddle repeated. "I ain't afraid to die. For I been thinkin'—since I been lyin' here, sick and alone—I been thinkin' that us mistakes has a good deal——"

The boy bent close.

"Comin' to us!"

The sunlight was climbing the bed-post.

"I been lookin' back," Mr. Poddle repeated. "Things don't look the same. You gits a bird's-eye view of life—from your deathbed. And it looks—somehow—different."

There was a little space of silence—while the Dog-faced Man drew long breaths: while his wasted hand wandered restlessly over the coverlet.

"You got the little brush, Richard?" he asked, his voice changing to a tired sigh. "The adornment has got in the way again."

The boy brushed back the fallen hair—wiped away the sweat.

"Your mother," said Mr. Poddle, faintly smiling, "does it better. She's used—to doing it. You ain't—done it—quite right—have you? You ain't got—all them hairs—out of the way?"

"Yes."

"Not all," Mr. Poddle gently persisted; "because I can't—see—very well."

While the boy humoured the fancy, Mr. Poddle lay musing—his hand still straying over the coverlet: still feverishly searching.

"I used to think, Richard," he whispered, "that it ought to be done— in public." He paused—a flash of alarm in his eyes. "Do you hear me, Richard?" he asked.

"Yes."

"Sure?"

"Oh, yes!"

Mr. Poddle frowned—puzzled, it may be, by the distant sound, the muffled, failing rumble, of his own voice.

"I used to think," he repeated, dismissing the problem, as beyond him, "that I'd like to do it—in public."

The boy waited.

"Die," Mr. Poddle explained.

A man went whistling gaily past the door. The merry air, the buoyant step, were strangely not discordant; nor was the sunshine, falling over the foot of the bed.

"'Last Appearance of a Famous Freak!'" Mr. Poddle elucidated, his eyes shining with delight—returning, all at once, to his old manner. "Git me, Richard?" he continued, excitedly. "'Fitting Finale! Close of a Curious Career! Mr. Henry Poddle, the eminent natural phenomonen, has consented to depart this life on the stage of Hockley's Musee, on Sunday next, in the presence of three physicians, a trained nurse, a minister of the gospel and a undertaker. Unparalleled Entertainment! The management has been at unprecedented expense to git this unique feature. Death Defied! A Extraordinary Educational Exhibition! Note: Mr. Poddle will do his best to oblige his admirers and the patrons of the house by dissolving the mortal tie about the hour of ten o'clock; but the management cannot guarantee that the exhibition will conclude before midnight.'" Mr. Poddle made a wry face—with yet a glint of humour about it. "'Positively,'" said he, "'the last appearance of this eminent freak. No return engagement.'"

Again the buoyant step in the hall, the gaily whistled air—departing: leaving an expectant silence.

"Do it," Mr. Poddle gasped, worn out, "in public. But since I been lyin' here," he added, "lookin' back, I seen the error. The public, Richard, has no feelin'. They'd laugh—if I groaned. I don't like the public—no more. I don't want to die—in public. I want," he concluded, his voice falling to a thin, exhausted whisper, "only your mother—and you, Richard—and — —"

"Did you say—Her?"

"The Lovely One!"

"I'll bring her!" said the boy, impulsively.

"No, no! She wouldn't come. I been—in communication—recent. And she writ back. Oh, Richard, she writ back! My heart's broke!"

The Mother

The boy brushed the handkerchief over the Dog-faced Man's eyes.

"'Are you muzzled,' says she, 'in dog days?'"

"Don't mind her!" cried the boy.

"In the eyes of the law, Richard," Mr. Poddle exclaimed, his eyes flashing, "I ain't no dog!"

The boy kissed his forehead—there was no other comfort to offer: and the caress was sufficient.

"I wish," Mr. Poddle sighed, "that I knew how God will look at it—to-night!"

Mr. Poddle, exhausted by speech and emotion, closed his eyes. By and by the boy stealthily withdrew his hand from the weakening clasp. Mr. Poddle gave no sign of knowing it. The boy slipped away.... And descending to the third floor of the tenement, he came to the room where lived the Mexican Sword Swallower: whom he persuaded to return with him to Mr. Poddle's bedside.

They paused at the door. The woman drew back.

"Aw, Dick," she simpered, "I hate to!"

"Just this once!" the boy pleaded.

"Just to say it!"

The reply was a bashful giggle.

"You don't have to *mean* it," the boy argued. "Just *say* it—that's all!"

They entered. Mr. Poddle was muttering the boy's name—in a vain effort to lift his voice. His hands were both at the coverlet—picking, searching: both restless in the advancing sunshine. With a sob of self-reproach the boy ran quickly to the bedside, took one of the wandering hands, pressed it to his lips. And Mr. Poddle sighed, and lay quiet again.

"Mr. Poddle," the boy whispered, "she's come at last."

There was no response.

"She's come!" the boy repeated. He gave the hand he held to the woman. Then he put his lips close to the dying man's ear. "Don't you hear me? She's come!"

Mr. Poddle opened his eyes. "Her—massive—proportions!" he faltered.

"Quick!" said the boy.

"Poddle," the woman lied, "I love you!"

Then came the Dog-faced Man's one brief flash of ecstasy— expressed in a wondrous glance of joy and devotion: but a swiftly fading fire.

"She loves me!" he muttered.

"I do, Poddle!" the woman sobbed, willing, now, for the grotesque deception. "Yes, I do!"

"'Beauty,'" Mr. Poddle gasped, "'and the Beast!'"

They listened intently. He said no more.... Soon the sunbeam glorified the smiling face....

HIS MOTHER

While he waited for his mother to come—seeking relief from the melancholy and deep mystification of this death—the boy went into the street. The day was well disposed, the crowded world in an amiable mood; he perceived no menace—felt no warning of catastrophe. He wandered far, unobservant, forgetful: the real world out of mind. And it chanced that he lost his way; and he came, at last, to that loud, seething place, thronged with unquiet faces, where, even in the sunshine, sin and poverty walked abroad, unashamed.... Rush, crash, joyless laughter, swollen flesh, red eyes, shouting, rags, disease: flung into the midst of it—transported from the sweet feeling and quiet gloom of the Church of the Lifted Gross—he was confused and frightened....

A hand fell heartily on the boy's shoulder. "Hello, there!" cried a big voice. "Ain't you Millie Blade's kid?"

"Yes, sir," the boy gasped.

It was a big man—a broad-shouldered, lusty fellow, muscular and lithe: good-humoured and dull of face, winning of voice and manner. Countenance and voice were vaguely familiar to the boy. He felt no alarm.

"What the devil you doing here?" the man demanded. "Looking for Millie?"

"Oh, no!" the boy answered, horrified. "My mother isn't—*here!*"

"Well, what you doing?"

"I'm lost."

The man laughed. He clapped the boy on the back. "Don't you be afraid," said he, sincerely hearty. "I'll take you home. You know me, don't you?"

"Not your name."

"Anyhow, you remember me, don't you? You've seen me before?"

"Yes, sir."

"Well, my name's Jim Millette. I'm an acrobat. And I know you. Why, sure! I remember when you was born. Me and your mother is old friends. Soon as I seen you I knew who you was. 'By gad!' says I, 'if that ain't Millie Slade's kid!' How is she, anyhow?"

"She's very well."

"Working?"

"No," the boy answered, gravely; "my mother does not work."

The man whistled.

"I am living with Mr. Fithian, the curate," said the boy, with a sigh. "So my mother is having—a very good—time."

"She must be lonely."

The boy shook his head. "Oh, no!" said he. "She is much happier— without me."

"She's *what*?"

"Happier," the boy repeated, "without me. If she were not," he added, "I would not live with the curate."

The man laughed. It was in pity—not in merriment. "Well, say," he said, "when you see your mother, you tell her you met Jim Millette on the street. Will you? You tell her Jim's been—married. She'll understand. And I guess she'll be glad to know it. And, say, I guess she'll wonder who it's to. You tell her it's the little blonde of the Flying Tounsons. She'll know I ain't losing anything, anyhow, by standing in with that troupe. Tell her it's all right. You just tell her I said that everything was all right. Will you?"

"Yes, sir."

"You ain't never been to a show, have you?" the man continued. "I thought not. Well, say, you come along with me. It ain't late. We'll see the after-piece at the Burlesque. I'll take you in."

"I think," said the boy, "I had better not."

"Aw, come on!" the acrobat urged.

"I'm awful glad to see you, Dick," he added, putting his arm around the boy, of kind impulse; "and I'd like to give you a good time—for Millie's sake."

The boy was still doubtful. "I had better go home," he said.

"Oh, now, don't you be afraid of me, Dick. I'll take you home after the show. We got lots of time. Aw, come on!"

It occurred to the boy that Providence had ordered events in answer to his prayer.

"Thank you," he said.

"You'll have a good time," the acrobat promised. "They say Flannigan's got a good show."

The Mother

They made their way to the Burlesque. Flannigan's Forty Flirts there held the boards. "Girls! Just Girls! Grass Widows and Merry Maids! No Nonsense About 'Em! Just Girls! Girls!" The foul and tawdry aspect of the entrance oppressed the child. He felt some tragic foreboding....

Within it was dark to the boy's eyes. The air was hot and foul—stagnant, exhausted: the stale exhalation of a multitude of lungs which vice was rotting; tasting of their very putridity. A mist of tobacco smoke filled the place—was still rising in bitter, stifling clouds. There was a nauseating smell of beer and sweat and disinfectants. The boy's foot felt the unspeakable slime of the floor: he tingled with disgust.

An illustrated song was in listless progress. The light, reflected from the screen, revealed a throng of repulsive faces, stretching, row upon row, into the darkness of the rear, into the shadows of the roof—sickly and pimpled and bloated flesh: vicious faces, hopeless, vacuous, diseased. And these were the faces that leered and writhed in the boy's dreams of hell. Here, present and tangible, were gathered all his terrors. He was in the very midst of sin.

The song was ended. The footlights flashed high. There was a burst of blatant music—a blare: unfeeling and discordant. It grated agonizingly. The boy's sensitive ear rebelled. He shuddered.... Screen and curtain disappeared. In the brilliant light beyond, a group of brazen women began to cavort and sing. Their voices were harsh and out of tune. At once the faces in the shadow started into eager interest—the eyes flashing, with some strangely evil passion, unknown to the child, but acutely felt.... There was a shrill shout of welcome—raised by the women, without feeling. Down the stage, her person exposed, bare-armed, throwing shameless glances, courting the sensual stare, grinning as though in joyous sympathy with the evil of the place, came a woman with blinding blonde hair.

It was the boy's mother.

"Millie!" the acrobat ejaculated.

The Mother

The boy had not moved. He was staring at the woman on the stage. A flush of shame, swiftly departing, had left his face white. Presently he trembled. His lips twitched—his head drooped. The man laid a comforting hand on his knee. A tear splashed upon it.

"I didn't know she was here, Dick!" the acrobat whispered. "It's a shame. But I didn't know. And I—I'm—sorry!"

The boy looked up. He called a smile to his face. It was a brave pretense. But his face was still wan.

"I think I'd like to go home," he answered, weakly. "It's—time—for tea."

"Don't feel bad, Dick! It's all right. *She's* all right."

"If you please," said the boy, still resolutely pretending ignorance, "I think I'd like to go—now."

The acrobat waited for a blast of harsh music to subside. The boy's mother began to sing—a voice trivially engaged: raised beyond its strength. A spasm of distress contorted the boy's face.

"Brace up, Dick!" the man whispered. "Don't take it so hard."

"If you please," the boy protested, "I'll be late for tea if I don't go now."

The acrobat took his hand—guided him, stumbling, up the aisle: led him into the fresh air, the cool, clean sunlight, of the street.... There had been sudden confusion on the stage. The curtain had fallen with a rush. But it was now lifted, again, and the dismal entertainment was once more in noisy course.

It was now late in the afternoon. The pavement was thronged. Dazed by agony, blinded by the bright light of day, the boy was roughly jostled. The acrobat drew him into an eddy of the stream. There the child offered his hand—and looked up with a dogged little smile.

"Good-bye," he said. "Thank you."

The acrobat caught the hand in a warm clasp. "You don't know your way home, do you?" he asked.

"No, sir."

"Where you going?"

The boy looked away. There was a long interval. Into the shuffle and chatter of the passing crowd crept the muffled blare of the orchestra. The acrobat still held the boy's hand tight—still anxiously watched him, his face overcast.

"Box Street?" he asked.

"No, sir."

"Aw, Dick! think again," the acrobat pleaded. "Come, now! Ain't you going to Box Street?"

"No, sir," the boy answered, low. "I'm going to the curate's house, near the Church of the Lifted Cross."

They were soon within sight of the trees in the park. The boy's way was then known to him. Again he extended his hand—again smiled.

"Thank you," he said. "Good-bye."

The acrobat was loath to let the little hand go. But there was nothing else to do. He dropped it, at last, with a quick-drawn sigh.

"It'll come out all right," he muttered.

Then the boy went his way alone. His shoulders were proudly squared—his head held high....

The Mother

Meantime, they had revived Millie Slade. She was in the common dressing-room—a littered, infamous, foul, place, situated below stage. Behind her the gas flared and screamed. Still in her panderous disguise, within hearing of the rasping music and the tramp of the dance, within hearing of the coarse applause, this tender mother sat alone, unconscious of evil—uncontaminated, herself kept holy by her motherhood, lifted by her love from the touch of sin. To her all the world was a temple, undefiled, wherein she worshipped, wherein the child was a Presence, purifying every place.

She had no strength left for tragic behaviour. She sat limp, shedding weak tears, whimpering, tearing at her finger nails.

"I'm found out!" she moaned. "Oh, my God! He'll never love me no more!"

A woman entered in haste.

"You got it, Aggie?" the mother asked.

"Yes, dear. Now, you just drink this, and you'll feel better."

"I don't want it—now."

"Aw, now, you drink it! Poor dear! It'll do you lots of good."

"He wouldn't want me to."

"Aw, he won't know. And you need it, dear. *Do* drink it!"

"No, Aggie," said the mother. "It don't matter that he don't know. I just don't want it. I *can't* do what he wouldn't like me to."

The glass was put aside. And Aggie sat beside the mother, and drew her head to a sympathetic breast.

"Don't cry!" she whispered. "Oh, Millie, don't cry!"

"Oh," the woman whimpered, "he'll think me an ugly thing, Aggie. He'll think me a skinny thing. If I'd only got here in time, if I'd only looked right, he might have loved me still. But he won't love me no more—after to-day!"

"Hush, Millie! He's only a kid. He don't know nothing about—such things."

"Only a kid," said the mother, according to the perverted experience of her life, "but still a man!"

"He wouldn't care."

"They *all* care!"

Indeed, this was her view; and by her knowledge of the world she spoke.

"Not him," said Aggie.

The mother was infinitely distressed. "Oh," she moaned, "if I'd only had time to pad!"

This was the greater tragedy of her situation: that she misunderstood.

NEARING THE SEA

It was Sunday evening. Evil-weather threatened. The broad window of top floor rear looked out upon a lowering sky—everywhere gray and thick: turning black beyond the distant hills. An hour ago the Department wagon had rattled away with the body of Mr. Poddle; and with the cheerfully blasphemous directions, the tramp of feet, the jocular comment, as the box was carried down the narrow stair, the last distraction had departed. The boy's mother was left undisturbed to prepare for the crucial moments in the park.

She was now nervously engaged before her looking-glass. All the tools of her trade lay at hand. A momentous problem confronted her. The child must be won back. He must be convinced of her worth. Therefore she must be beautiful. He thought her pretty. She would be pretty. But how impress him? By what appeal? The pathetic? the tenderly winsome? the gay? She would be gay. Marvellous lies occurred to her—a multitude of them: there was no end to her fertility in deception. And she would excite his jealousy. Upon that feeling she would play. She would blow hot; she would blow cold. She would reduce him to agony—the most poignant agony he had ever suffered. Then she would win him.

To this end, acting according to the enlightenment of her kind, she plied her pencil and puffs; and when, at last, she stood before the mirror, new gowned, beautiful after the conventions of her kind, blind to the ghastliness of it, ignorant of the secret of her strength, she had a triumphant consciousness of power.

"He'll love me," she thought, with a snap of the teeth. "He's got to!"

Jim Millette knocked—and pushed the door ajar, and diffidently intruded his head.

"Hello, Jim!" she cried. "Come in!"

The man would not enter. "I can't, Millie," he faltered. "I just got a minute."

"Oh, come on in!" said she, contemptuously. "Come in and tell me about it. What did you do it for, Jim? You got good and even, didn't you? Eh, Jim?" she taunted. "You got even!"

"It wasn't that, Millie," he protested.

"Oh, wasn't it?" she shrilled.

"No, it wasn't, Millie. I didn't have no grudge against you."

"Then what was it? Come in and tell me!" she laughed. "You dassn't, Jim! You're afraid! come in," she flashed, "and I'll make you lick my shoes! And when you're crawling on the floor, Jim, like a slimy dog, I'll kick you out. Hear me, you pup? What you take my child in there for?" she cried. "Hear me? Aw, you pup!" she snarled. "You're afraid to come in!"

"Don't go on, Millie," he warned her. "Don't you go on like that. Maybe I *will* come in. And if I do, my girl, it won't be me that'll be lickin' shoes. It might be *you*!"

"Me!" she scorned. "You ain't got no hold on me no more. Come in and try it!"

The man hesitated.

"Come on!" she taunted.

"I ain't coming in, Millie," he answered. "I didn't come up to come in. I just come up to tell you I was sorry."

She laughed.

"I didn't know you was there, Millie," the man continued. "If I'd knowed you was with the Forty Flirts, I wouldn't have took the boy there. And I come up to tell you so."

Overcome by a sudden and agonizing recollection of the scene, she put her hands to her face.

"And I come up to tell you something else," the acrobat continued, speaking gently. "I tell you, Millie, you better look out. If you ain't careful, you'll lose him for good. He took it hard, Millie. Hard! It broke the little fellow all up. It hurt him—awful!"

She began to walk the floor. In the room the light was failing. It was growing dark—an angry portent—over the roofs of the opposite city.

"Do you want him back?" the man asked.

"Want him back!" she cried.

"Then," said he, his voice soft, grave, "take care!"

"Want him back?" she repeated, beginning, now, by habit, to tear at her nails. "I got to have him back! He's mine, ain't he? Didn't I bear him? Didn't I nurse him? Wasn't it me that—that—*made* him? He's my kid, I tell you—*mine*! And I want him back! Oh, I want him so!"

The man entered; but the woman seemed not to know it. He regarded her compassionately.

"That there curate ain't got no right to him," she complained. "*He* didn't have nothing to do with the boy. It was only me and Dick. What's he sneaking around here for—taking Dick's boy away? The boy's half mine and half Dick's. The curate ain't got no share. And now Dick's dead—and he's *all* mine! The curate ain't got nothing to do with it. We don't want no curate here. I raised that boy for myself. I didn't do it to give him to no curate. What right's he got coming around here—getting a boy he didn't have no pain to bear or trouble to raise? I tell you *I* got that boy. He's mine—and I want him!"

"But you give the boy to the curate, Millie!"

"No, I didn't!" she lied. "He took the boy. He come sneaking around here making trouble. *I* didn't give him no boy. And I want him back," she screamed, in a gust of passion. "I want my boy back!"

A rumble of thunder—failing, far off—came from the sea.

"Millie," the acrobat persisted, "you said you wasn't fit to bring him up."

"I ain't," she snapped. "But I don't care. He's mine—and I'll have him."

The man shrugged his shoulders.

"Jim," the woman said, now quiet, laying her hands on the acrobat's shoulders, looking steadily into his eyes, "that boy's mine. I want him—I want him—back. But I don't want him if he don't love me. And if I can't have him—if I can't have him——"

"Millie!"

"I'll be all alone, Jim—and I'll want——"

He caught her hands. "Me?" he asked. "Will you want me?"

"I don't know."

"Millie," he said, speaking hurriedly, "*won't* you want me? I've took up with the little Tounson blonde. But *she* wouldn't care. You know how it goes, Millie. It's only for business. She and me team up. That's all. She wouldn't care. And if you want me—if you want me, Millie, straight and regular, for better or for worse—if you want me that way, Millie——"

"Don't, Jim!"

He let her hands fall—and drew away. "I love you too much," he said, "to butt in now. But if the boy goes back on you, Millie, I'll come—again. You'll need me then—and that's why I'll come. I don't want him to go back on you. I want him to love you still. It's because of the way you love him that I love you—in the way I do. It ain't easy for me to say this. It ain't easy for me to want to give you up. But you're that kind of a woman, Millie. You're that kind—since you got the boy. I want to give you up. You'd be better off with him. You're—you're—*holier*—when you're with that child. You'd break your poor heart without that boy of yours. And I want you to have him—to love him—to be loved by him. If he comes back, you'll not see me again. I've lived a life that makes me—not fit—to be with no child like him. But so help me God!" the man passionately declared, "I hope he don't turn you down!"

"You're all right, Jim!" she sobbed. "You're all right!"

"I'm going now," he said, quietly. "But I got one more thing to say. Don't fool that boy!"

She looked up.

"Don't fool him," the man repeated. "You'll lose him if you do."

"Not fool him? It's so easy, Jim!"

"Ah, Millie," he said, with a hopeless gesture, "you're blind. You don't know your own child. You're blind—you're just blind!"

"What you mean, Jim?" she demanded.

"You don't know what he loves you for."

"What does he love me for?"

The man was at the door. "Because," he answered, turning, "you're his mother!"

It was not yet nine o'clock. The boy would still be in the church. She must not yet set out for the park. So she lighted the lamp. For a time she posed and grimaced before the mirror. When she was perfect in the part, she sat in the rocking-chair at the broad window, there to rehearse the deceptions it was in her mind to practice. But while she watched the threatening shadows gather, the lights on the river flash into life and go drifting aimlessly away, her mind strayed from this purpose, her willful heart throbbed with sweeter feeling—his childish voice, the depths of his eyes, the grateful weight of his head upon her bosom. Why had he loved her? Because she was his mother! A forgotten perception returned to illuminate her way—a perception, never before reduced to formal terms, that her virtue, her motherly tenderness, were infinitely more appealing to him than the sum of her other attractions.

She started from the chair—her breast heaving with despairing alarm. Again she stood before the mirror—staring with new-opened eyes at the painted face, the gaudy gown: and by these things she was now horrified.

"He won't love me!" she thought. "Not this way. He—he—couldn't!"

It struck the hour.

"Nine o'clock!" she cried. "I got to *do* something!"

She looked helplessly about the room. Why had he loved her? Because she was his mother! She would be his mother—nothing more: just his mother. She would go to him with that appeal. She would not seek to win him. She would but tell him that she was his mother. She would be his mother—true and tender and holy. He would not resist her plea.... This determined, she acted resolutely and in haste: she stripped off the gown, flung it on the floor, kicked the silken heap under the bed; she washed the paint from her face, modestly laid her hair, robed herself anew. And when again, with these new, seeing eyes, she looked into the glass, she found that she was young, unspoiled—still lovely: a sweetly wistful woman, whom he resembled. Moreover, there came to transform her, suddenly, gloriously, a revelation: that of the spiritual significance of her motherhood.

"Thank God!" she thought, uplifted by this vision. "Oh, thank God! I'm like them other people. I'm fit to bring him up!"

It thundered ominously.

THE LAST APPEAL

She sat waiting for him at the bench by the lilac bush. He was late, she thought—strangely late. She wondered why. It was dark. The night was close and hot. There was no breath of air stirring in the park. From time to time the lightning flashed. In fast lessening intervals came the thunder. Presently she caught ear of his step on the pavement—still distant: approaching, not from the church, but from the direction of the curate's home.

"And he's not running!" she thought, quick to take alarm.

They were inexplicable—these lagging feet. He had never before dawdled on the way. Her alarm increased. She waited anxiously — until, with eyes downcast, he stood before her.

"Richard!" she tenderly said.

"I'm here, mother," he answered; but he did not look at her.

She put her arms around him. "Your mother," she whispered, while she kissed him, "is glad—to feel you—lying here."

He lay quiet against her—his face on her bosom. She was thrilled by this sweet pressure.

"Have you been happy?" she asked.

"No."

"Nor I, dear!"

He turned his face—not to her: to the flaming cross above the church. She had invited a question. But he made no response.

"Nor I," she repeated.

Still he gazed at the cross. It was shining in a black cloud—high in the sky. She felt him tremble.

"Hold me tight!" he said.

She drew him to her—glad to have him ask her to: having no disquieting question.

"Tighter!" he implored.

She rocked him. "Hush, dear!" she crooned. "You're safe—with your mother. What frightens you?"

"The cross!" he sobbed.

God knows! 'twas a pity that his childish heart misinterpreted the message of the cross—changing his loving purpose into sin. But the misinterpretation was not forever to endure....

The wind began to stir the leaves—tentative gusts: swirling eagerly through the park. There was a flash—an instant clap of thunder, breaking overhead, rumbling angrily away. Two men ran past. Great drops of rain splashed on the pavement.

"Let us go home," the boy said.

"Not yet!" she protested. "Oh, not yet!"

He escaped from her arms.

"Don't go, Richard!" she whimpered. "Please don't, dear! Not yet. I—I'm—oh, I'm not ready to say good-night. Not yet!"

He took her hand. "Come, mother!" he said.

"Not yet!"

He dropped her hand—sprang away from her with a startled little cry. "Oh, mother," he moaned, "don't you want me?"

"Home?" she asked, blankly. "Home—with me?"

"Oh, yes, mother! Let me go home. Quick I Let us go.... The curate says I know best. I went straight to him—yesterday—and told him. And he said I was wiser than he.... And I said good-bye. Don't send me back. For, oh, I want to go home—with you!"

She opened her arms. At that moment a brilliant flash of lightning illuminated the world. For the first time the child caught sight of her face—the sweet, real face of his mother: now radiant, touched by the finger of the Good God Himself.

"Is it you?" he whispered.

"I am your mother."

He leaped into her arms—found her wet eyes with his lips. "Mother!" he cried.

"My son!" she said.

He turned again to the flaming cross—a little smile of defiance upon his lips. But the defiance passed swiftly: for it was then revealed to him that his mother was good; and he knew that what the cross signified would continue with him, wherever he went, that goodness and peace might abide within his heart. Hand in hand, while the thunder still rolled and the rain came driving with the wind, they hurried away towards the Box Street tenement....

Let them go! Why not? Let them depart into their world! It needs them. They will glorify it. Nor will they suffer loss. Let them go! Love flourishes in the garden of the world we know. Virtue is forever in bloom. Let them go to their place! Why should we wish to deprive the unsightly wilderness of its flowers? Let the tenderness of this mother and son continue to grace it!

THE END

Lightning Source UK Ltd.
Milton Keynes UK
UKHW010638310521
384676UK00001B/97

9 781006 933103